DEADHORSE EXPRESS

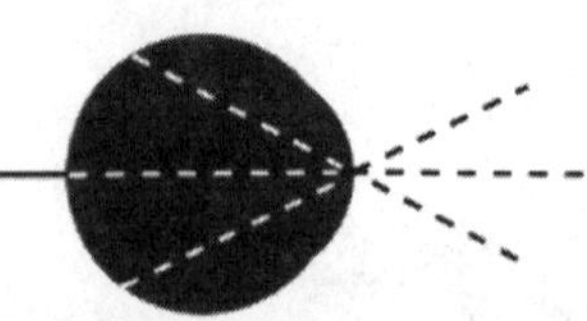

DEADHORSE EXPRESS

Walker A. Tompkins

CENTER POINT LARGE PRINT
THORNDIKE, MAINE

This Center Point Large Print edition is published
in the year 2016 by arrangement with
Golden West Literary Agency.

First US edition: Phoenix Press.
First UK edition: Hutchinson.

The text of this Large Print edition is unabridged.
In other aspects, this book may vary
from the original edition.
Printed in the United States of America
on permanent paper.
Set in 16-point Times New Roman type.

ISBN: 978-1-68324-080-8 (hardcover)
ISBN: 978-1-68324-084-6 (paperback)

Library of Congress Cataloging-in-Publication Data

Names: Tompkins, Walker A., author.
Title: Deadhorse express / Walker A. Tompkins.
Description: Center Point Large Print edition. | Thorndike, Maine :
Center Point Large Print, 2016.
Identifiers: LCCN 2016021978 | ISBN 9781683240808
(hardcover : alk. paper)
Subjects: LCSH: Large type books. | GSAFD: Western stories.
Classification: LCC PS3539.O3897 D427 2016 | DDC 813/.54—dc23
LC record available at https://lccn.loc.gov/2016021978

To
C. E. Tompkins
and
Bertha Tompkins

DEADHORSE EXPRESS

—Chapter I—

Killer's Toll Bridge

Deadhorse town took to cover and peered from behind its windows as gun-hung Bret Redfern swaggered out on the canyon bridge to station himself for a showdown.

The big miner planted his boots wide apart and hooked thumbs in the shell belts which girdled his massive body. He scowled toward the steep road that snaked down from the Badluck Mountains which overhung the town.

Cattle choked that cut-out trail from edge to edge. Cattle bearing the Rocking R brand of the big Arizona syndicate that had trailed the herd for hundreds of miles across Nevada's desert to gain this mining-camp destination.

The steers had weathered the grueling miles surprisingly well; mute testimony, for men with cow savvy, to the skill of the sombreroed punchers who were now hazing the bawling mass of beef toward the Death Canyon bridge which linked the badlands with Deadhorse town.

In the vanguard of the dusty caravan of longhorns rode a lean, slit-eyed puncher whom Bret Redfern knew would be the trail boss in control of the north-bound Rocking R herd. Hal Wade would be his name, if Redfern's advance information had been correct.

A trail boss capable of delivering six hundred head of spooky longhorns to the Comstock Lode country without letting their ribs show through the tallow would be a hard man, a shrewd leader of an equally hard crew.

Not a man, Bret Redfern knew, who would be disposed to submit kindly to a toll bridge which was the only barrier between his herd and a hard-worn trail's end.

And now, as Hal Wade drew rein a dozen yards from the heavy log bridge and swung his gaze toward the weather-beaten signboard which Redfern had erected on the opposite rimrock, Redfern knew by the thrust of Wade's jaw and the cold lights behind slitted eyelids that his advance size-up of the Rocking R boss was true.

In breath-held suspense, the hidden population shifted their gaze between Bret Redfern and the mounted rider who pointed the oncoming herd.

No change came across Wade's dust-grimed face as he read the signboard and considered its import:

WELCOME TO DEADHORSE
Private Bridge
Bret Redfern, Tollmaster
PAY TOLL AT GATE!

Bret Redfern stalked slowly forward, meeting the impact of the trail boss' stare. A hundred feet below the bridge, plunging waters marked Death River's turbulent channel over tumbled and jagged rock.

"You aimin' to bring that stock acrost here, stranger?"

Hal Wade thrust a trail-dusty Stetson back on his head, to reveal a plainer view of a saddle-brown face deeply lined by hard days in wind and weather.

"If this is the closest way to get to Cal Bozeman's corrals, I reckon I am."

Redfern's flashing eyes went beyond Wade to where the oncoming steers were bunching between the narrow cutbanks. Horn hit horn in deafening clatter amid an undertone of cloven hoofs on rubble. The shrill yips of cowboys sounded above the sullen roar of bawling cattle. That herd smelled water, the first in twelve hours. They would not be easy to stop.

"How many flitter-ears does that herd tally, Wade?"

The Arizona trail boss dismounted and stood sliding the reins through his rope-calloused hands.

"Roughly six hundred. If you're Bozeman, you can check 'em as they go through the gates."

"I ain't Bozeman. My name's Redfern. It'll cost you two bits a head to cross this bridge. You and your crew can drift in without charge."

Wade's brows drew into a pucker as he calculated mentally the staggering toll which Redfern demanded.

"I got my doubts if Cal Bozeman would want to shell out a hundred and fifty bucks before my beefstuff gets in his pen. My contract reads to deliver those steers on the hoof at Bozeman's place. You and him can do the dickerin' on this toll-bridge business. Right now, I ain't aimin' to stop them cattle. I got my doubts if it could be done."

Redfern glanced over his shoulder. Out of the tail of his eye he saw Fanner Poleson, the ace gunslammer in his employ, moving casually out of Deadhorse's main street to back his play on the bridge.

"Stoppin' them cattle ain't my lookout, Wade," warned Redfern sharply. "Cough up a hundred and fifty simoleons or I shut the toll gate. And without no guard rails on this bridge, some of those boogery steers is li'ble to drop a long way before they hit the water they're sniffin'."

Wade looked behind him. The Rocking R cattle were down on the level road now. The leaders would soon be breaking into a trot. Hell or high water couldn't stop them short of the big log toll gate now, and a bunch-up on the narrow bridge would bring an inevitable slaughter in the canyon below, as Redfern had predicted.

"You don't own this bridge, Redfern. I found that out miles back. The gold miners built this bridge—"

Redfern's hairy arm dropped toward a thonged-down holster.

"But I own the ground on the Deadhorse side where the bridge ties to the rimrock, feller. People that try to cross without paying my toll don't find it healthy—"

Wade dropped his bridle reins and stepped away from his horse. He half turned and waved an arm in a come-ahead signal to his Rocking R punchers who were beginning to fan out in advance of the approaching herd.

Redfern had a six-gun half out of leather as the trail boss turned back to face the leering toll-master. But events were crowding too close behind Wade for the trail boss to bandy further talk.

With the same smooth motion of a rattlesnake's strike, Hal Wade's bunched knuckles shot out and up in a terrific punch which smashed through the thin scrub of beard on Redfern's jaw and paralyzed the nerve center there.

Arms windmilling, six-gun clattering on the hoof-splintered puncheons of the canyon toll bridge, the big miner staggered backward and then sprawled on his back.

Lifting his gaze from the stunned tollmaster, Hal Wade looked up to see Fanner Poleson halt in the act of swinging shut the heavy log toll gate beyond him.

Snarling an oath, the gunman dug for steel, his arm coming up with a Colt .45 that belched gray smoke.

A slug bit through Wade's left chap wing. Another sprayed wooden slivers over his boots as Poleson lined his Colt and got the range.

A lance of answering flame tore through the bore of Wade's six-gun as he triggered once, then holstered the gun and leaped to pick up Redfern's groaning bulk.

Without looking at the crumpling form of the killer at the half-closed toll gate, Wade boosted Redfern in jack-knife fashion over his saddle, then seized bit rings and led his horse forward to clear the bridge for the oncoming cattle herd.

Fanner Poleson, his chest drilled by Wade's single slug, collapsed over the top bar of the toll gate, his blood dripping in bright splashes over the puncheons.

The thundering hoofs of the longhorned leaders were reverberating on the opposite end of the bridge as Hal Wade led his horse and its moaning burden to the safety of Deadhorse's wide, twisting street.

By the time Wade had lowered Redfern to the ground, the Rocking R cattle were stampeding by in a russet flood, briskets swinging the corpse-draped toll gate wide as the Arizona steers milled down into the street.

As if oblivious of the brief gunplay he had weathered, the trail boss from the south forked his cow pony and began beating dusty cattle with a lariat end, to keep the flanks from breaking into the intersecting alleyways.

A din of sound roared through the mining camp as the Rocking R Syndicate's cattle herd raced in pandemonium through the narrow street, to where Cal Bozeman's corral gates yawned wide at the far edge of the town.

Yelling cowboys forced the longhorns into the receiving pen, where water troughs became jammed on the instant. A tally count would come later when the herd was admitted into the larger corral built against the mountainside.

A white-faced, bandy-legged hombre dressed in hickory shirt and a butcher's apron sought out Hal Wade where the latter had pulled up alongside the corral gate, his long job finished.

"I'm Bozeman," panted the stranger. "You shouldn't—"

"There's your steers, Bozeman!" yelled back Wade. "Even if you pay that tinhorn crook his toll, you'll cash in plenty selling fresh meat to these gold grubbers. They're fat and frisky as corn-fed critters from Kansas."

The gold-camp butcher rolled his eyes in horror.

"I ain't beefin' about the toll, amigo. But I seen that play you made agin' Bret Redfern at the bridge just now. He ramrods this burg, young feller—and you wrote yourself a one-way ticket to hell when you bucked him. Him and his gun-slick crew will make shore you don't git back to Rocking R range alive!"

—Chapter II—

Bad-Town Editor's Advice

The closing of Bozeman's corral gates on the bawling Arizona cattle herd was the signal for Deadhorse town to come to life.

Bat-wing doors on the saloons and gambling dives and false-fronted store buildings which rimmed the crooked main street swung open to disgorge roughly dressed, hard-bitten men who, in spite of their nervous panic, were strangely, ominously silent.

Hal Wade, if he noticed the electric tension that overhung the Nevada gold camp, gave no outward sign as he spurred over to where his dozen-odd riders had bunched alongside the receiving pens.

"It'll take a couple hours to tally up and get our pay from Bozeman, boys," announced the trail boss. "You've all got a little dinero in your pants, I reckon. High-tail it to a livery and bed down your hosses. By the time you cut the trail dust out of your craws and need some more cash, I'll have it for you. An' I can't blame you for doin' some celebratin'."

But where the Rocking R cowpunchers would ordinarily have thrown their sombreros aloft and split the air with raucous whoops at the prospect of going on a bender to celebrate the end of a long trail drive, the men received Wade's bantering dismissal with uneasy side glances and an air of suspense.

For weeks these riders had sweated and eaten and slept with reckless abandon, working desperately in desert wastes and tangled mountain passes under Wade's driving but respected discipline.

A scant third of them had witnessed Wade's characteristic disposal of the toll-gate barrier. But the others quickly heard about it and sensed the disaster which hung cloudlike over the town.

Out of sight up the street, Bret Redfern had picked himself up and disappeared. The corpse of Fanner Poleson was collecting blow flies over by the bridge gate, where gate and corpse had been flung aside by a brown tidal wave of trail-weary cattle.

With the prospect of fresh gunplay soon to come, no one in the town felt inclined to dispose of the dead man. And Hal Wade was too busy with Cal Bozeman's tally men to stop and consider the bombshell he had hurled into the tough camp.

He had time to consider it an hour later, when the last straggler had been hazed through counting chutes into fenced-in pasturage beyond Bozeman's corrals at the town's edge.

Cal Bozeman, smarter than most of the fortune-crazed men who had flooded this section of Nevada in quest of gold and silver, was carving out his own fortune in the lucrative and safer method of buying beefstuff wholesale and dispensing it to gold camps and Chinese restaurants at dizzy profits.

The Rocking R herd, fattening on meadow grass in outlying mountain corrals fenced in by beetling cliffs, would supply the wild town's meat throughout the coming fall and winter. But Cal Bozeman had no stomach for his prospective business as he guided Hal Wade into his modest office behind a log butcher shop on a side street.

"Tally was five hundred and ninety-two critters, according to my sheet," grunted Wade, dropping into a rawhide-bottomed chair as Bozeman seated himself behind a rickety desk. "Right?"

The wholesale butcher shoved aside his rumpled tally sheet.

"Forget the tally, Wade. Damn it, I feel like I'm paying off a dead man. Give me a receipt for this dust."

Bozeman swabbed perspiration from his moon-shaped face as he leaned down to twirl the dial of a rusty safe. Wade said:

"If you're worrying about me getting that gold dust back to the syndicate, forget it. They give me orders to ship it home by Wells Fargo stage. I ain't a fool to carry a young fortune in *oro* when the express outfit will insure it."

Bozeman turned from his safe to throw up his trembling hands in exasperation.

"What kind of a man are you, Wade?" groaned the butcher. "I ain't worryin' about the syndicate gettin' their money—that's your responsibility. But I hate to see a proddy young fool like you go to boothill ahead of your time."

Hal Wade fished makings from the crescent-shaped pocket of his orange shirt and began shaping a smoke.

He was in his early thirties, near as Bozeman could judge. His saddle-warped legs were incased in cactus-scuffed bat wings; and double gun belts encircled his middle, the ivory-mounted butts of .45 Peacemakers holstered at either hip.

Everything about him bespoke a long and hard trail—matted horsehair fouling his spur rowels, alkali dust caked thick on cowhide boots, the red bandanna looped about his throat was powdery with dust and grit.

"Listen to reason, Wade. You better let me turn this dust over to Wells Fargo for you. You lay low until dark and then light a shuck out of town by the back trail before you collect a dose of lead poisonin'."

Wade, licking his brownie thoughtfully, fixed the agitated butcher with a mildly cynical eye.

"I thought the way into—and out of—Deadhorse was over the Death Canyon bridge."

Licking his lips with something akin to desperation, Cal Bozeman opened his safe and drew out several pokes solid with gold dust—yellow metal mined from the surrounding hills, and in common use as legal tender throughout northern Nevada.

"I don't think you realize what you did when you killed Redfern's ace gun hawk, Wade," panted Bozeman, counting out the buckskin sacks. "Ain't you ever heard of Redfern? But you haven't—or you wouldn't have refused to pay his toll. Better men than you have tried that—which same accounts for Deadhorse having such a thriving cemetery."

Wade snapped flame from a match with his thumbnail and lighted his cigarette. Blue smoke purling from his nostrils, the Arizona trail boss answered:

"Them cattle were comin' hell bent for leather, Bozeman. If I'd let Redfern buffalo me, hard tellin' how many critters would have fell into the canyon."

Bozeman shoved a small pile of gold-dust pokes across the desk and handed Wade a receipt to sign. The meat dealer then got out balance scales, but Wade waved his hand and scrawled his signature on the paper.

"How about giving me the lowdown on this

Redfern hombre, Bozeman?" asked Wade as he picked up the pokes and stowed them in a saddle-bag. "Redfern hinted that he's a salty hombre, but that's just one man's opinion. Confidentially, now, what do you—"

Cal Bozeman hustled to the door of his shop. Turning on the top step, he waited until Wade had passed him and was on the street.

"Salty don't describe Redfern, young feller. An' don't come to me for info. Our transaction's finished—through—over with. I got my beef, you got your money—and a hell of a mess of trouble before they pour the clods over your coffin. And while you're at it, you better take a long squint at that sun over the Badlucks, Wade—because I got my doubts about you seein' it set."

Wade gave a mock wince as the door of Bozeman's establishment slammed a vehement period to the meat dealer's discourse. Picking up his reins, the trail boss headed thoughtfully out onto the main street of the gold camp, trailing his buckskin pony behind.

"A hell of a welcome for the hombre who's brought this burg the only fresh meat it'll have all winter," grunted Wade half facetiously. "And now, the sooner I can get this syndicate money salted away with Wells Fargo, I reckon the safer it'll be."

Deadhorse was similar to any one of a dozen Western settlements that Wade had encountered during the thirty-one turbulent years he had knocked around the border. Advance descriptions of the gold-rush town had not been exactly flattering; but that depended on a man's point of view, Wade reflected soberly.

The wildest town in Nevada? He had heard that superlative voiced frequently along the north trail. Not boastfully, but with the dread respect men reserve for topics like hellfire and stampedes and drought and violent death. All these elements, it would seem, were melted in the crucible of outlawry that was Deadhorse town; according to hearsay.

Wade was not the one to swallow hearsay gullibly. But now, as he made his slow advance up the once more deserted street, the prickling hairs on his neck nape told him that what he had heard regarding Deadhorse had not been exaggerated.

The torrid wind, gusting down off the Badluck ridges, rattled a warped signboard over a flimsy shack on his left, attracting his attention. The waddy's eyes lighted as he read the words which marked his first destination before hunting up a barn for his pony and a restaurant to fill his hungry vitals:

WELLS FARGO EXPRESS COMPANY
Curly Joyce, Agent

"Right over there, Jelly-ribs, is where we'll stow the syndicate's dinero," Wade told his horse as he tied up at a chewed cottonwood hitch rail in front of the stagecoach office. "Then we'll see about grainin' and groomin' you."

Shouldering his saddlebags, one of which sagged under the weight of the gold dust, Hal Wade ducked under the rail and trailed his spurs under the wooden awning of the Wells Fargo office.

A lone man slouched in the doorway, chewing a toothpick; a consumptive-looking specimen who was neither miner nor cowman, judging from the pallor of his face or the mysterious black stains on his fingers. A brown canvas apron draped about his middle told Wade that the man was a printer by trade, therefore not the Wells Fargo agent, Curly Joyce.

"You figuring to get Wells Fargo to transport that gold out of Deadhorse?" inquired the printer bluntly, toothpick waggling between thin, bloodless lips.

"Wells Fargo are in the business of packin' express, ain't they?" countered Wade, starting to shoulder past the lanky individual and then noting that the office door was locked.

The printer fixed Wade with a pale eye.

"Yes, an' no, son. As a friendly citizen of this here town, an' editor of its only newspaper, I'm in a position to say what I'm goin' to say about Wells Fargo."

"Meanin' what?"

"Meanin' that folks in this town who want their gold to get to its destination send it on stages belonging to Bret Redfern's express company. You've already had one brush with that skunk—but don't ride your luck too hard, Mr. Wade, because folks in this town are already layin' bets you won't ride out of this camp alive."

—Chapter III—

A Challenge—and Fire

Hal Wade shifted the weight of his gold-laden *alforja* bag on one shoulder and sized up the pallid-faced editor again. At least this ink-smeared printer had the guts to tell a stranger what he thought of Bret Redfern, and to do it openly on the public street. His very presence here in the doorway of the Wells Fargo office was in sharp contrast to the behavior of the rest of the town, who had once more taken to cover in anticipation of a shoot-out to come.

"You seem to know my name already," said Wade, pinching out his cigarette and grinding it under heel. "You bein' a newspaper hombre, maybe you can give me some dope about this Redfern. Supposin' we rattle our hocks over to that café yonder an' talk it over?"

The gangly printer shrugged indifferently, then fell in step beside Wade as the two crossed the wheel-rutted street toward a Chinaman's restaurant.

"I'm Jimmy O'Niel—editor an' owner of the *Weekly Observer*," said the cadaverous printer. "I been in Deadhorse ever since the first tent was pitched around these gold an' silver diggin's.

I know Bret Redfern's stripe, an' I smelt skunk oil on that walloper before he started squashin' this town under his heel."

Five minutes later, seated opposite each other, across a plain pine table, the pair had ordered beefsteak and spuds and coffee from a wrinkled Chinaman who shuffled off on slippered feet as if anxious to keep his distance from Wade.

Other customers in the place gulped down their coffee or left meals untouched on various excuses to get out of the establishment. These signs of taut-drawn nerves were not lost on the trail driver from the border country. He guessed their meaning even before Jimmy O'Niel of the *Observer* started unreeling a few of his observations.

"This Redfern—who is he?" asked Wade curiously. "Seems to ramrod this town like he owned it."

O'Niel nodded soberly.

"Redfern's an owl-hooter. Only man in town with authority to buck him is Rocky Donovan, the marshal—but Redfern operates too slick for Donovan to pin any murder or robbery or other skullduggery on him. It's a sour story, Wade—"

"Sour" was hardly the adjective, Wade had cause to reflect a few minutes later. He learned why Deadhorse town feared and hated—and obeyed—Bret Redfern.

Redfern owned the Lucky Lode, richest-paying

mine in the Badluck area. Likewise he owned the Blue Skull, largest gambling dive and saloon in town. Less than a year before, Redfern had expanded his greedy enterprises by forming the Thunderbolt Express Co., running stagecoaches, mail and freight to Carson City.

"He's all but crowded out Wells Fargo," O'Niel continued. "Curly Joyce is a salty character, but it's useless to buck Redfern. Curly's stage-coaches get held up so often they've nicknamed 'em the 'Boothill Express.' Often as not, Curly loses a driver or guard."

"I'd admire to meet up with Curly Joyce," mused Wade. "Is Redfern behind those holdups and killings?"

"Figger it out for yourself, Wade. It ain't very often *Redfern's* coaches git held up—unless Injuns attack. But Curly Joyce's Boothill Express have an uphill grade all the way."

Hal Wade rubbed his stubborn jaw thoughtfully. Men who knew the Rocking R trail boss read in that gesture a danger signal that Wade habitually made before going into action.

"I've decided," Wade said slowly, "to ship by Wells Fargo, as the syndicate ordered me to do. If Curly Joyce is willin' to take my shipment, I'll gamble on it gettin' through—even if I have to ride guard on his Boothill Express myself."

The shuffling Chinaman returned from the kitchen, his almond eyes widened with alarm.

"No got spluds, coffee, bleefsteak today," stammered the Oriental lamely. "Cowboy mebbeso go somewhere else, mebbe?"

Wade's ice-blue eyes glinted with humor.

"I get it," he chuckled. "You figger Bret Redfern's on the prowl, aimin' to hunt me up so's he'll be able to resume the business we left unfinished out by the toll bridge?" asked the cowboy.

The Chinaman nodded, rubbing his long-nailed fingers together in trembling anxiety.

"Wing Sing no have dead man in place yet, you sabby? Wing Sing no want guns bleak up dishes, mebbeso bleak up windowglass—"

The shaky-voiced restaurant owner broke off, his slanted eyes staring in horror at the front door. Then, with a squall of fear, the Chinese fled into his kitchen in a flurry of apron, his greased queue flapping snakelike behind him.

Hal Wade straightened, peering at the front door. A towering man in an undertaker's frock coat and with a long, horselike face had just entered. His eyes, bleak and fishlike as a corpse's orbs, raked the interior of Wing Sing's eating house and came to rest on the man from Arizona.

"That's Black Bill Collier, Redfern's right-hand man," whispered Jimmy O'Niel, twisting uneasily on the pine bench. "Showdown's on the way, Wade, so keep your shootin' irons loose."

Black Bill Collier stalked across the restaurant

floor, the flowing tails of his black coat showing the bulges of twin six-guns belted beneath them.

"You tied a knot in Bret Redfern's tail a couple hours ago, Wade!" clipped the gunman, halting beside Wade's table. "He's give you time to get your affairs in order. Now he's waitin' for you out on the street in front of the Blue Skull Bar."

Jimmy O'Niel, watching the cowboy's face apprehensively, saw no change in color, no muscular twitch or other change in expression. Yet he knew that Black Bill Collier's words had been a death sentence relayed to him by the heartless gun boss of the mining camp.

"You go back an' tell your yellow-bellied boss that Hal Wade ain't in the habit of goin' *to* anybody to settle arguments, Collier!" replied the Rocking R foreman coolly. "Right now I'm hungry. If Bret Redfern wants to see me, he damn well knows where I am without sendin' a flunky after me."

Purple wrath flooded Collier's bony features. Then he composed himself and bowed mockingly.

" '*Sta bueno*," the gun hawk answered. "It ain't any skin off my nose how you commit suicide. I'll deliver your message. I'd fulfill any reasonable request—from a dyin' man."

Collier's coattails swirled about his lean legs as the saloon tough wheeled and left the restaurant. Hal Wade, craning his neck toward the kitchen, saw Wing Sing's saffron face pressed against a tiny glass window in the door. Then the Chinaman disappeared, and Wade heard the sound of a back door slamming on Wing Sing's retreat.

"Looks like I got to fight a duel with an empty belly, O'Niel," chuckled Wade, rising. "I reckon there's other restaurants in this camp."

O'Niel shrugged laconically and fished a grimy sheaf of proof papers from his vest pocket.

"By the way, Wade—what's your home address?" the printer asked casually. "I always like to keep my obituary notices accurate. They're the first thing folks read in the *Observer.*"

Wade laughed at the grim portent of O'Niel's words.

"You're gettin' premature, O'Niel. I'm six foot two, in case you specialize in coffin measurements. But I aim to live to a ripe old age—so ripe I'll be damned near rotten. Let's go."

Jimmy O'Niel remained at Wade's side until they reached the doorway opening on the street. There he paused, gripping the waddy by one elbow.

"I got a paper to git out," he said. "Reckon you better go the rest of the way *solo.* And good luck, kid."

Hal Wade tensed inwardly as he stepped out on the splintery sidewalk. He knew that O'Niel expected ambush shots to ring out. But Wade, with a keen knowledge of men, believed he had Redfern ticketed for a killer who would fight his own battles—especially when he had been publicly humiliated. Redfern, for all his ruthlessness, would not be a coward. Thereby he would be doubly dangerous to have as a foeman.

Wade glanced up and down the street, expecting to see the menacing figure of Bret Redfern somewhere near, waiting to goad him into a six-gun duel.

Even as he looked around, Wade caught sight of Bret Redfern walking toward him, a hundred yards up the street. No other man was visible, but Redfern's bullish figure was easily recognized. Redfern advanced with shoulders hunkered in a gunman's crouch.

And then, from an unexpected quarter, an interruption occurred to postpone the inevitable clash.

A low, muffled explosion sounded somewhere near at hand, and simultaneously there issued a bellowing shout:

"Fire! *Fire!* Wells Fargo's place is burnin' up!"

Magically, the streets began filling with men, blotting out the stalking figure of Bret Redfern.

Hal Wade, swinging his gaze to the left, started violently as he saw a mushrooming pall of ugly black smoke billowing out of attic windows on the Wells Fargo depot across the street.

Red flames guttered behind closed windows. Coils of sooty vapor were seeping through cracks in the shingles, pouring thickly under the raftered eaves.

In a Western town of closely packed buildings built of flimsy clapboards, roofed with canvas or tarpaper or tinder-dry shingles, a fire was a devastating thing.

Men raced out of a gambling hall next door to the Wells Fargo Express building to splash buckets of water on the walls as protection against the moment when the holocaust inside the stagecoach depot would break through the walls and endanger surrounding structures.

Then, above the raucous yells of men and the sullen roar of the fire which was gutting the interior of the Wells Fargo shack, came a staccato clatter of horse's hoofs.

Charging at reckless speed down the center of the street came a girl, wearing a flat-topped Stetson and a man's Levi's. She sawed violently on the reins and leaped running from her clay-bank pony, even as she came opposite the blazing stage depot.

Hal Wade, stepping off the sidewalk into fetlock-deep dust, saw the girl race past the hitch rail where Wade's own bronc was bucking violently with panic. She sped up the Wells Fargo steps, tried the door, then peered through the glass panel above the knob.

Then her scream smote Wade's eardrums, even as she jerked a key from her pocket and unlocked the stagecoach office:

"Dad's in there! Oh, dad's in there—"

She flung open the door, staggered back from a blast of heated air. Then, pulling a neckerchief over her face, the girl ducked inside the shack and was lost behind a roiling curtain of pink-and-gray and pitch-black smoke.

—Chapter IV—

The Extraordinary Curly Joyce

Hal Wade, sprinting across the street to rescue his cow pony from the vicinity of the fire, ducked on under the hitch rail and under the wooden awning of the doomed shack.

Men yelled hoarse warnings as the cowboy adjusted his own bandanna neckerchief about his face and plunged into the smoke and flame.

Heat singed his eyebrows, blasted his body with almost a physical impact as he peered frantically about. The opened doorway served as a forced draft to feed the blaze that seemed to be consuming floor and walls and ceiling all at once.

Dimly through clouds of smoke Wade saw the girl, kneeling behind an overturned table over a prostrate body.

It was the figure of a man in shirt sleeves, whose face was a bloody mask from a deep gash over one temple. Instantly Hal Wade knew that he was looking at Curly Joyce, the only man in Deadhorse who had had the courage to buck the six-gun dictator of the gold diggings.

"He's worth saving, even if he ain't alive!" thought Wade, stumbling forward through the smoke and shoving the desperate girl to one side.

The girl looked up, and through the fiery heat and strangling smoke, Hal Wade saw her thank him with her eyes.

She stumbled back as Wade hoisted the inert body of Joyce over his shoulders, on top of the saddlebags already hanging there.

"Got to get out pronto!" Wade shouted, seizing the girl's arm and fighting his way toward the door. "This place'll be cavin' in before another couple of ticks—"

Lurching under the burden of the heavy Wells Fargo agent, Hal Wade staggered out of the door and into an area of oven-heated but smokeless air outside.

Shoving the girl toward the hitch rack, he yelled against her ear:

"Yuh'll oblige me by untyin' that buckskin, miss. He's my hoss."

Before Wade had carried Joyce out to the middle of the street, the girl had led Wade's leggy saddler, Jelly-ribs, out to where her own claybank pony waited.

"This way—to Doc Phelps' office!" came the girl's high-pitched cry.

Wide-eyed townsmen shuttled their gaze between the spectacular picture of the flame-enveloped Wells Fargo office and the equally dramatic spectacle of the Arizona cowboy toting his limp burden down the street.

With a crash, the Wells Fargo shack tumbled into ruins like a house of cards, its fire-eaten rafters plunging to the floor and the charred walls folding up on top of the blazing wreckage.

A moment later Wade was carrying the unconscious Joyce into a wooden-floored tent, across whose canvas fly had been painted the words: *Zebediah Phelps, M. D. Gunshot Wounds A Specialty.*

As if he had anticipated their arrival, the bald-headed old medico led Wade to a rear room and stripped back a blanket from a white-sheeted cot.

The girl hovered over the unconscious man as Dr. Phelps and Wade deposited her father on the bed. Then, with quick professional orders to the girl and Wade, Doc Phelps went into action.

The girl brought a tea kettle of boiling water from a nearby stove; Wade, hustling to obey Phelps' instructions, found clean linen bandages in a wall cabinet.

"Your dad ain't bad hurt—just slugged on the noggin with a gun butt," said the doctor, busy with antiseptic and cotton. "Must have been layin' low on the floor where the smoke hadn't settled, because he ain't coughin'. An' his pulse is strong."

Ten minutes later, when the Wells Fargo agent was sputtering back to consciousness and the girl was holding a teaspoon of whiskey between his lips, Hal Wade made his way to the canvas-partitioned front room of the doctor's tent.

He found a washbasin and was cleaning soot from his face and eyes when he felt a touch on his arm and turned to see Joyce's daughter standing beside him, tears brimming in her eyes as she extended a strong, sun-tanned hand to clasp his.

"I . . . I wanted to thank you . . . for what you did," she whispered brokenly. "I couldn't have dragged dad out of there in time. We both would have burned to death . . . and no one else in this rotten town would have come inside and helped me."

Wade grinned awkwardly, feeling suddenly self-conscious before her frank gaze. She was beautiful, he found himself thinking; beautiful and feminine, in spite of her mannish dress and the deep, even tan of her skin. If her glossy roan hair had been tucked under the flat-crowned sombrero, she would have passed for a man. Her handclasp was strong.

"I know who you are," she panted. "I guess everyone in Deadhorse knows who you are . . . after what happened . . . at the bridge. But why . . . should you risk your life . . . for strangers like us—"

Wade squared his shoulders and brushed ashes from his shirt and the wings of his chaps. He jerked a thumb toward the other room, where the Wells Fargo agent was getting a turbanlike bandage wrapped around his head.

"It wasn't . . . just because I saw a girl in

danger . . . that I went in there, Miss Joyce," answered the cowboy. "But I'd heard about your father. Curly Joyce an' me have got somethin' in common, even if we don't know each other. Curly Joyce is buckin' Redfern—the only man in town with the g—with the nerve to stand up an' talk back to Redfern."

A strange expression played in the girl's eyes as he finished speaking.

"You thought my father was Curly Joyce?"

Wade's fire-seared brows arched in surprise.

"Why, I reckoned so, yes. He's the Wells Fargo agent—"

A smile flickered over the girl's carmine lips.

"He's assistant agent. He's my father, Rex Joyce. Got crippled up during a stagecoach robbery, and now he tends to the office work."

"Then Curly Joyce—the hombre who's buckin' Redfern—"

Good humor replaced the haunting anxiety in the girl's eyes.

"To call Curly Joyce an 'hombre' would be a little funny. You see, I'm Curly Joyce."

The cowboy's jaw widened with startled wonder. He glanced into the back room, where Rex Joyce was sitting up in the bed, gulping at a whiskey glass in Dr. Phelps' hand. Then Wade's gaze came back to this laughing girl in man's clothing, a girl with a businesslike Colt .45 holstered at one hip.

"*You*—Curly Joyce? You mean a . . . a *girl* is handling the Wells Fargo job in this hell-bent town?"

Before Curly Joyce could answer, Rex Joyce clumped through the canvas partition to stare wild-eyed at his daughter.

"That was Redfern's work, burnin' us out, Curly!" panted the old man. "I was takin' a nap, last I remember. Doc says somebody sneaked up an' slugged me—"

Curly Joyce nodded, a bitter light kindling in her eyes.

"I know. And the reason our place burned so fast was because that shipment of kerosene for the mercantile store was dumped all around the place. Redfern's determined to stamp Wells Fargo out of business if he has to kill us to do it."

Dr. Phelps joined them, briskly wiping his hands on a towel.

"Yes, and you'll both move out of Deadhorse before it's too late, if you take my advice!" rasped the medico. "This is like all of Redfern's dirty work. You haven't a clue to work on."

Curly Joyce stepped over to her father and gripped his hands.

"Dad, I want you to meet Hal Wade, the man who . . . who saved both our lives," she said, turning about. "Mr. Wade—"

She broke off as she saw that the man from Arizona was no longer inside the doctor's tent.

—Chapter V—

Donovan Breaks It Up

Outside, Hal Wade was pushing his way to the doctor's hitch rail where Curly Joyce had tied his buckskin pony.

He had arrived in Deadhorse in time to witness the tragic climax of the war between rival express outfits; and from what he had seen and heard, Bret Redfern held aces to the girl's deuces.

Strapping his gold-laden saddlebags behind the cantle, Wade mounted and spurred through the crowd which was being compressed back before the fevered blast of heat from the crumbling heap of ashes and charred timber that had been the Wells Fargo shack.

A bucket brigade of red-shirted miners and townsmen were saving adjacent buildings while the crowd looked on. But Hal Wade was spurring his saddler on through the congested, milling throng, making in the direction of a false-fronted shack on whose paint-pealed boards had been painted a huge blue skull.

Above it was the word "Saloon"; below it the legend he had been seeking: "Bret Redfern, Prop."

The burly gun boss of the gold camp was

standing on the porch of his deserted establishment, along with a pair of white-aproned bartenders who served double duty as bodyguards, judging from the gun harness whose bulk showed through the aprons.

Deadhorse's population, unaware that showdown was crystallizing beyond the fire zone, made no attempt to clear the streets or to gain vantage points from which to watch a gun duel in safety. They were absorbed in the grim business of keeping the Wells Fargo fire from spreading and wiping out the town.

"I got your message, Redfern!" called out Hal Wade as he reined up his buckskin in front of the Blue Skull. "Sorry I was delayed—but I had some business to attend to back yonder a piece."

Redfern's head motioned imperceptibly and the barkeeps faded from view behind green slatted doors. Redfern, apparently, intended to settle his issue with Wade personally; or else wanted his gun-toting backers in ambush in case Hal Wade proved too fast on the draw.

"So I see." Redfern's voice was laconic, steel-edged.

Redfern was a big man; his size was even more striking, now that Wade had a chance to size him up. He towered six feet two, the same as Wade himself; but he outweighed the rangy cowpoke by a good eighty pounds.

He reminded Wade, somehow, of a grizzly.

There was no extra fat on those muscle-slabbed bones; the hidden strength of steel trap seemed to lurk in Redfern's tapered, knobby fingers.

As befitted the kingpin of Deadhorse diggings, Bret Redfern went in for flash, as might a gambler. A huge gold chain hung suspended across a flowered waistcoat; his six-guns were trimmed in silver mined from his own stopes in nearby hills; and two tiny diamonds had been set in Redfern's bucklike front teeth, glittering curiously when the man's thick lips peeled back on a grin of mirth, or derision as now.

"Leavin' town?" inquired Redfern, rubbing a shoulder against a pillar of his tar-roofed porch.

Wade's eyes were bleak as he shook his head.

"Yes an' no, Redfern. I'm leavin' tomorrow mornin' on the outbound Wells Fargo stage. Accordin' to your flunky, Collier, you an' me got an account to square up before I dust out of Deadhorse. That's why I'm here."

Redfern's evil face, fringed with unshaven, scrubby beard, flooded with color as he stepped down off his porch, hands wide at his side, as if poised for throwing the silver-mounted .45s at his thighs.

"You may leave town on the Wells Fargo wagon tomorrow," he said, "but you won't enjoy the trip. You won't even see the scenery. You—"

A jangle of spur chains halted Redfern even as he and Wade faced each other for shoot-out. Both men looked up the street to see a short, chunky-built hombre approaching them at a casual gait. On the newcomer's black vest gleamed a five-pointed star engraved with the single word, "Marshal."

Without appearing to observe that he had interrupted a peril-fraught moment, that his arrival had forestalled sudden death for one or both of the men he faced, the lawman halted midway between Redfern and Wade.

Bret Redfern relaxed, as if muscle by muscle was slumping within him as tension eased. Without a word the gunman turned on his heel and walked into his Blue Skull barroom.

"I'm Rocky Donovan, the marshal," clipped the lawman. "Just come from Dr. Phelps' tent. Curly Joyce wants to see you."

Wade nodded his thanks and reined his buckskin back up the street. Rocky Donovan, thumbs hooked in armpits, remarked after him in a casual tone which would not reach listening ears inside the Blue Skull:

"Forget your idea of hoorawin' Bret Redfern, son. That's my business. Even if you'd beat him to the draw just now, you wouldn't have done anything for Deadhorse town. Redfern's got as many men backin' his crooked play as a porcupine has quills."

Wade lifted a rope-calloused hand in token of thanks.

"*Bueno*, Donovan. I may take your advice—an' mebbe I won't."

He skirted through a back alley behind a blacksmith shop to avoid the throng engaged in putting out the Wells Fargo fire. Approaching Dr. Phelps' tent from the rear, he dismounted and entered the tent to find Curly Joyce and her father still discussing their recent loss with the sympathetic old sawbones.

"Oh—Mr. Wade!" said the girl, her face lighting at Wade's entrance. "You got away before dad or myself had a chance to thank you—"

Wade dismissed her outburst with a wave of his hand.

"Forget that, Miss Joyce. You got a stagecoach leavin' for Carson City tomorrow?"

She nodded. "And I'm the jehu that'll be driving it," she said, with what Wade thought was a defiant upthrust of chin. "Our only other driver, Whip Gleason, won't be in with our other Concord until tomorrow."

Wade grinned, as if in eagerness at her news.

"Fine. I got a consignment of gold dust to ship out with your Boothill Express, miss. Belongs to the cattle syndicate I work for—the Rocking R, in Arizona."

The girl considered his words gravely.

"Boothill Express—then you've heard the . . . the reputation our company has—and still want to trust us with your gold dust?"

Wade's hands unconsciously dropped to rub his gun stocks.

"I figger to be settin' on the driver's seat with you, Miss Joyce. As a sort of shotgun guard, you might say. Any objections?"

Curly Joyce looked at her father and back to Wade again. Then she impulsively thrust out a slim, strong hand.

"It's a deal, Wade!" she said determinedly. "Dad almost had me talked into giving up my Wells Fargo agency. But I reckon tomorrow's Boothill Express will get through!"

—Chapter VI—

Rimrock Disaster

An uneasy undercurrent of excitement gripped Deadhorse town that night as news sped about the gold camp by the mysterious grapevine system of the frontier which made even the least important news common knowledge long before Jimmy O'Niel could set it into type for his *Weekly Observer.*

Tonight's news was double-edged in its suspense. Curly Joyce, hard-fighting, hard-riding, straight-shooting girl of the badlands would be taking out the early-morning Concord for Carson City, in open defiance of Redfern's latest and most crushing blow against the Wells Fargo—the fire and attempted murder of Rex Joyce.

Equally as important as the girl's defiant action of the morrow was the still-pending clash between Redfern and Hal Wade, the Arizona cowboy who had been unheard of in Deadhorse prior to his arrival in the gold camp.

Bets were being laid that night in Redfern's Blue Skull poker palace at even odds that Hal Wade would not live through the night. Other gamblers throughout the town, learning of Wade's intention to ride guard on the Wells Fargo Concord, sought to bet any amount that the latest Boothill Express would not get out of Death River Pass, but could get no takers.

Bret Redfern, glowering behind the imported oaken desk of his headquarters in the rear of the Blue Skull Saloon, where he handled the activities of his Lucky Lode mining interests and his Thunderbolt Express Co., heard the news of Hal Wade's stage-guard job from the lips of his chief henchman, Black Bill Collier.

Redfern grunted cryptically.

"Curly keeps her stagecoach in the Silver Nugget livery barn," grunted the outlaw. "I'm depending on you, Collier, to damage a wheel, savvy? Curly's asked for war, so she'll get it, woman or no woman. You know what to do. It was just tough luck you didn't get Rex Joyce when you set fire to his shack today."

Redfern turned back to his papers and ledgers, and when he glanced up again, Black Bill Collier had departed.

Collier indeed "knew what to do." Bret Redfern had gained his diabolical grip on the mining, saloon and express business of Deadhorse by employing his brains more frequently than force.

At no time had the forces of law and order in the gold camp—as exemplified in the person of Rocky Donovan—been able to hang a crime on Redfern's doorstep.

As in the case of that afternoon's destruction of the Wells Fargo Express depot—a blow calculated to drive Curly Joyce and her stagecoaches out of Nevada forever—there was never a tangible clue to point an accusing finger at Bret Redfern.

Men did not challenge his right to exact heavy tolls whenever an ore-laden string of mules crossed the Death Canyon bridge; freight wagoneers paid tribute in cash to Redfern, not without complaint, but certainly without opposing him outwardly with gun or fist.

Not, that is, until the arrival on the scene of Hal Wade, that cool-voiced and mild-mannered hombre from the Rocking R beef syndicate down south.

Black Bill Collier knew that Hal Wade was spending the night in the Bonanza Hotel, within six-gun range of the Blue Skull. But Redfern was not so crude as to hire his gun hawks to murder Wade in his sleep.

It was typical of Redfern's fiendish ingenuity that he had figured out a way to be rid of the menace, however temporary, of Hal Wade, at the same time he destroyed Curly Joyce and the Wells Fargo competition she represented.

Collier waited, therefore, until well after midnight before venturing forth to obey his chief's instructions. Then, keeping to dark alleyways, he made his path to the Silver Nugget Livery Stable, in a rear shed of which Curly Joyce's Wells Fargo stagecoaches were sheltered.

Dimly in the gloom Collier saw the outlines of the stagecoach, its wheels and bolsters painted a canary yellow, its paneled body vermilion.

Making his way to the side of the stagecoach which Curly Joyce and Hal Wade would be taking out on the arrival of daylight, Collier hunted through a tool box and obtained a heavy wrench.

With this he carefully loosened the hubcap of the right front wheel of the Concord and removed the heavy cotter pin which kept the wheel bolt on the axle.

He screwed the hubcap until only a few threads held it in place and smeared the axle heavily with black grease from a can in the stagecoach tool box. Then, to make his deception complete, Collier dusted the tampered hub with powdery soil found underfoot.

That done, Redfern's henchman returned to his sleeping quarters in the attic of the Blue Skull and retired to sleep the sleep of a man untroubled by twinges of a conscience that had long since been dulled by evil.

Hal Wade, emerging triumphantly from Wing Sing's Chinese eating house next morning with a good breakfast in his stomach, found half the population of Deadhorse and surrounding gold fields on hand to see the morning Boothill Express off for Carson City.

A hostler at the Silver Nugget had already loaded

his saddle on the roof of the Concord. His gold dust was in Curly's strongbox.

Six horses, bearing the Wells Fargo brand, were ready in the traces. As Wade shouldered his way through the strangely silent crowd surrounding the stage, he saw Curly Joyce already mounting into the driver's seat, flat-crowned Stetson perched at a jaunty angle above her coppery tresses, braided chin cord holding it in place.

A sawed-off shotgun rested on the boot beside her. Her even white teeth flashed in a smile of greeting as the Concord jounced on its leather thoroughbraces and as Hal Wade mounted the seat beside her.

Tied to the rear of the canvas-booted coach, by means of a hempen hackamore, was Jelly-ribs, Wade's leggy buckskin.

"All ready to roll, pardner?" laughed the girl, picking up her leather ribbons with one hand and leaning forward to take whip from socket with the other.

Wade, scanning the sea of sombreroed faces below and about them, nodded absently. All his Rocking R cowboys were in that mob; he had paid them off the night before, and most of them were bleary-eyed from their all-night carousal in Deadhorse's pleasure spots.

"Let 'er roll, Curly," responded the cowboy, easing his six-guns in their holsters and picking up the sawed-off buckshot gun. "Seems like everybody's on hand to tell us *adios*—except Bret Redfern's crowd."

The girl nodded grimly.

"We may meet up with them later—out in the Badlucks," she said in an undertone. "It isn't like Redfern to let this stage roll to Carson City without a fight."

Curly Joyce cracked her long, leather-thonged whip like a pistol shot, and the horses lunged in their traces. With a staggering lurch, the Concord rattled forward, the crowd of silent onlookers spreading a wide aisle before them as the leaders wheeled out onto the rutted street.

"So long, Curly!"

"Don't be a damned fool, Curly! You ought to know Red—you ought to know you can't git through!"

The girl appeared not to hear the clamor of voices, each one of which seemed to be pleading with her to cancel her run. From the corner of her eye she saw her father and Dr. Phelps, the former swathed in bandages, as they waved good-by from the doctor's tent.

Then, in a flurry of dust and with five-foot rear wheels clattering noisily, the Boothill Express rolled out across the Death's Canyon toll bridge—significantly open, and without the usual toll taker on duty.

The Concord contained no passengers. As Curly Joyce had informed Wade the night before, miners no longer dared ride out of the diggings with Wells Fargo. Redfern's Thunderbolt Express, it seemed, presented a surer and safer way of egress to the outside world, and consequently seized one hundred percent of the passenger trade.

Raucous yells came from Wade's Rocking R trail riders as the Concord gathered speed and headed off up the steep grade into the Badluck Mountains.

A moment later the cowboy, twisting in the seat to wave to Deadhorse town—a town he never expected to visit again—saw the clustering shacks disappear as the Concord topped the grade.

Wade, settling himself in the seat with boots braced against the scarred footboard, shot a sidelong glance at the firm-muscled girl beside him, managing the careening six-horse span with a cool skill that bespoke long experience.

A girl stage driver! Wade doubted if the West had ever seen that phenomenon before. It took physical prowess and a stubborn courage to hold down that job, even without the ever-present threat of ambush attack or raiding Indians.

The grade was steep, and Curly Joyce's left boot rode the rusty brake pedal when the lurching Concord threatened to overtake the rumps of the pounding wheel horses.

To their right was the precipitous gorge of Death River, water plunging in a foamy wash far below the rock-fanged cliff walls. The stage road hugged the rimrock with inches to spare; Wade knew its terrors, for he and his Rocking R crew had hazed six hundred head of restive longhorns up that route only the day before.

He leaned over the edge of the stage, intending to look back through the funneling dust to make sure that Jelly-ribs, his buckskin saddler, was trailing all right at the hackamore's end.

Then it was that Hal Wade caught sight of the right front wheel wobbling perilously on its axle, saw the metallic hubcap spin off to go bouncing off through the rocks and brush at cliff crest.

Too late, he turned to Curly Joyce to warn the girl that her Concord was losing a wheel at their dizzy gait down the steep grade. Even as he turned, the wheel spun from its axle and went bounding, like a thrown hoop, off through space and catapulting down into the blue gulf of the canyon at their right elbow.

"We lost a wheel, pard—jump while you can—"

Curly Joyce disregarded Wade's frantic yell as she felt the Concord teeter dizzily on three wheels.

She jammed the brake shoes against screaming steel tires, but it was futile, useless.

Her eyes met Wade's in a wild, brief instant of horror and knowledge of their doom as the hurtling Wells Fargo coach careened violently out of the ruts and tumbled its right front corner through the thin barricade of weeds which furred the Death Canyon rimrock.

"Jump, Curly—to the road—"

The dragging weight of the crippled stagecoach yanked squealing horseflesh from the road in a tangle of harness.

Out into empty space hurtled the overturning coach, deadly cliff wall blurring alongside them in their mad plunge—

Upside down in space, the crippled coach exposed its floorboards to the sky.

Like straw-stuffed dummies, Wade and the girl driver were hurtled deep into the canyon's abyss.

Then stagecoach, snorting team, Wade's horse, flying rocks, saddle, torn brush and dust—all plummeted toward the surging mountain torrent which Redfern had plotted to receive them in the embrace of a ghastly eternity.

—Chapter VII—

Courage to Carry On

Rushing gray-green waters soared up to meet Hal Wade's catapulting form as he was hurled free of the plummeting Wells Fargo stage and team.

Cliffs blurred past in a confused rush during the brief, mad plunge, giving him no time to kick his body into diving position, allowing him no glimpse of the girl who, an instant before, had been seated at his side on the crippled stagecoach.

The icy waters of Death River closed about the Arizonan with a clap of sound, more spray rising high to join the water still spouting upward from the impact of the Concord.

Instinct alone sealed the cowboy's lungs as Wade smacked into the rushing river.

He felt his spurred boots touch bottom, scraping along smooth, bowllike stone which untold centuries of scouring waters had gouged out of the granite walls.

Current tugged at his body, overcoming the bogging burden of shell belts and heavy .45 Peacemaker Colts which remained, as if by magic, clasped in leathern holsters.

He opened his eyes in icy water, for a

kaleidoscopic glimpse of opaque depths dimly lighted by the shafting rays of Nevada sunlight which penciled into the narrow gorge from the rimrocks fifty feet above.

A smashed wagon wheel floated with uncanny suspension not a dozen inches from his face.

The blurred, misty coach showed dimly through swirling waters as he was lifted toward the surface of the tumbling river by the speeding current.

Then he broke surface, to gasp in reviving air. Again instinct came to his aid, preventing him from sinking again into strangling depths from which there might be no return.

The surface of the river was littered with smashed panelling and other debris from the wrecked stage.

Even as he looked frantically about for a trace of Curly Joyce, the Arizona cowman saw the stage-coach itself rear to the surface in a surge of foam.

The threshing six-horse team had broken free of the stage. One of the wheel horses and both swing-span animals had been crippled by their impact with submerged rocks.

But the leaders, snorting with panic, were already swimming, dragging a tangle of harness, broken single-trees and the snapped-off wagon tongue behind them.

The canyon was a torrent of sound; as an eddy whipped him about in a semicircle, sweeping him toward a nearby smooth-walled cliff, Hal

Wade saw the tumbling, lacy wall of a seventy-foot cascade immediately to the east.

That waterfall—he remembered having seen it and admiring it on the trail drive only yesterday—had been responsible for the gouged-out depths into which he and Curly Joyce and their sabotaged Concord stagecoach had plunged. Elsewhere along Death Canyon's pit, saw-tooth boulders and foam-drenched rapids would have brought speedy and terrible death.

He swam, hard strokes fighting against the agony of bruised muscle and strained joints.

Downstream, beyond floating wreckage and swimming horses, Death River sloped at a gentle angle to disappear into a pothole from which pounding spray lifted in smokelike clouds, indicating another, and shorter waterfall.

In memory's flash, Hal Wade recalled a terrifying picture of those lower falls. Talus rock had crumbled from the overhanging rocks to clog and dam the foot of that second cataract.

In the split second of time following his return to the surface, Wade thought that a taunting fate had spared his life for the moment, only to sweep him to a grisly end at the foot of the lower falls.

A high-pitched, treble scream caused Wade to turn his head sharply around, in the direction of the floating wreckage.

A surge of relief swept him as he saw Curly

Joyce swimming with stout strokes a few feet nearer midstream.

It seemed impossible that the girl could have survived the mad plunge from the roof of the toppling stagecoach a moment before; but her blanched face was alive with expression and recognition as she spotted him, swimming in the grip of the current beside her.

The girl's strength was fast ebbing, however. Even as converging eddies brought them closer, Wade saw panic glaze Curly Joyce's eyes, saw her arms falter in midstroke, saw the weight of her buckskin skirt and heavy gun belt bog her down.

With desperate effort, Hal Wade cut down the intervening yards of racing water.

He thrust out an arm, felt her fingers clasp in his. Booming spray from a nearby boulder slammed his face as he gained momentary respite in a whirlpool, and increased the strength of his grip on the girl's hand.

Then he had seized her wrist, regained a grip on her forearm.

He tried to yell, but the thunder of the Upper Falls made speech impossible. Even the pitiful snorts of the wounded and swimming horses was lost on their eardrums, though the struggling team was near at hand.

The white clouds of smokelike vapor from the Lower Falls were coming closer now, with incredible speed. The surface of Death River was turning glassy-green, as the terrific suction of the drop-off in the river's bed forced the ripples to flatten out before the stream dropped over the Lower Falls.

Curly Joyce, her face a white blob through the spray and her spun-copper hair plastered wetly to her skull, was trying to disengage herself from Wade's grip; he could feel that, though the words her mouth was framing were unintelligible in the roar of cascading waters.

Bare seconds had elapsed since their plunge from the stage road overhead; but they seemed like eternity.

Only moments remained before they would be swept over the Lower Falls, in a tangle of broken stagecoach parts, harness, floating wheels and seat-cushion stuffing.

Wade knew that fighting the current was impossible. Yet he struggled desperately to keep the fainting girl's head above water, wondering why he did not give her the merciful alternative of unconsciousness before both of them were funneled into the narrowing channel of the waterfall's crest.

Then he found himself snatching at leather ribbons that coiled, snakelike, about him.

Through bulging eyes he saw that the six-horse team had lashed out to shallower water; the leaders were digging their hoofs into gravel, fighting to drag the dead swing-span horses and the struggling wheelers out of the main current.

He had a grip on the lines which Curly Joyce's fingers had released an instant before she was hurtled off the dropping stage.

He felt the leather ribbons go taut, felt his body and Curly's swept around in a bone-stretching arc as the horses anchored steel-shod hoofs in firm, water-smoothed stones.

Powerful horseflesh would be their only chance of cheating the Lower Falls of what seemed their inevitable human prey.

Desperately, Wade wrapped his forearm about two slippery lines.

Now they were being struck by the full force of the river's current, but their onward, downstream motion had halted.

The powerful drag of the Lower Falls was sucking at their legs, almost stripping boots from their feet. But the sturdy Wells Fargo span was winning its fight against the force of water and the pull of two human forms.

Inch by inch, Wade felt his body being towed out of the grip of the central current as the horses fought their way in a tangle of snarled harness out onto the near bank.

Curly Joyce's consciousness seemed restored by the agony of a wrenched arm socket, as Wade clung doggedly to her forearm while his other hand clutched the strained and glistening leather lines.

For horrifying seconds it appeared to Wade that

he must let go his hold, lest his elbow snap apart under the strain. He felt his grip on Curly Joyce's wrist beginning to weaken; he dug his fingers deeper into her flesh.

Then the bite of the current diminished; side currents seemed to push them, with a chagrined and jealous gesture, toward the safety of the bank up which the lead horses were dragging their fellows in a tangle of chains and broken traces.

The menace of the Lower Falls was slackening now. The horses, bending briskets into the staunch collars with the tenacity of draft animals pulling an unpullable load, fought their way up to a grassy ledge a few feet above the rocky shore.

Not until he and Curly Joyce had been towed and skidded into ankle-deep water did Hal Wade release his faltering hold on the harness lines that had saved their lives.

Struggling to his feet, the cowboy stooped to lift Curly Joyce in his arms. Giddiness from the pressure of strain threatened to overcome him, but a wan smile flickering over the girl's lips gave him courage to carry on.

A moment later he pitched forward on grassy refuge, rolling sideways to protect Curly Joyce from injury.

The brief, mad exploit was over. The stagecoach vanished unseen, in a flurry of sprinters over the Lower Falls. But the two human souls who had been the only passengers aboard that doomed Concord were safe.

—Chapter VIII—

Hot Lead Payoff

They made their way, a half hour later, down a spray-slippery ledge that took them to the broad base of the canyon at the foot of the Lower Falls.

Neither had spoken, during the twenty minutes it had taken them to recover their breath and take stock of themselves. Both had escaped broken bones or serious laceration. Yet neither man nor girl could bring themselves to look at the sharp, broken rocks heaped at the foot of the waterfall.

In silence, they stood on a sandy bank and looked down at what remained of the Wells Fargo stage. The undercarriage, shiny in lemon-colored paint, was strewn along the river bank for a quarter of a mile in the distance. The shell of the coach was reduced to kindling wood, nearby.

Stranded on a sandbar some distance below the waterfall was the carcass of Jelly-ribs, the buckskin cow pony Hal Wade had raised from a colt. Its neck had been snapped by the impact of its dive off the rimrock; it had been cruelly broken by the rocks at the base of the roaring cascade of the Lower Falls.

Curly Joyce, wringing out her hair and trying to

restore her buckskin blouse to some semblance of order, saw the haunting grief in Wade's eyes as he contemplated the dead body of his horse.

Without speaking to her, Wade skidded down the cutbank to where the bulk of the Concord stage had washed ashore. Under what was left of the driver's seat, behind tattered leather curtains, he fished out the tiny iron-bound Wells Fargo strong box.

Hoisting it to his shoulder, he scrambled back up the bank and dropped the treasure box at her feet.

"Anyway, your Rocking R gold shipment isn't lost," she said, eyes resting on the Wells Fargo emblem on the locked chest.

Wade removed his Colt .45s from holsters, jacked open the cylinders, and blew river water from the bores.

"And we're safe. That's what counts."

She looked up quickly, surprised at the tone in which he had couched the phrase.

"Three of your horses are stove up, Curly," he said quickly. "I'll take care of 'em."

He made his way over to where the trembling horses had halted, too shaken and exhausted by their swim to pay attention to the lush, bluestem grass that grew, fetlock deep, about them.

Curly Joyce looked the other way as three sharp, whiplike gunshots rang out and reverberated down the canyon, sounding a requiem for the swing-span pair and the crippled wheel horse.

Then Wade unhitched the living horses from the broken harness, turned the remaining wheeler loose and led the glistening leaders over to her side.

After he had strapped the Wells Fargo strong box to one of the hames on the off horse, he helped Curly to mount. Then he followed suit on the remaining horse.

"You figger that wheel come off by accident, Curly?"

The girl smiled mirthlessly as he voiced the question that had been in his mind ever since he had seen the tampered wheel wobbling on its axle, as prelude to disaster.

"Redfern—or one of the cowards who wear his collar—fixed that wheel, Hal."

Their eyes met in a level, penetrating glance.

"What you intend doing about it, Curly?"

Her jaw squared at the challenge in his voice.

"Stick it out, of course—and fight."

His voice was grave and gentle as they spurred the two stage horses into a trot, following a broken ledge which would bring them to the stagecoach road above.

"You're fightin' heavy odds, Curly. Too heavy —for a woman to be buckin' alone."

She squared her shoulders resolutely.

"I'm not alone. Dad's backing my play. Whip

Gleason is one of the saltiest reinsmen who ever tooled a Concord—as good as any jehu who ever cracked a whip. And Deadhorse—I've got plenty of friends there, Hal. Jimmy O'Niel, of the *Observer.* And lots of others—who'd patronize Wells Fargo, if they dared."

Wade did not speak again until their struggling horses had gained the stagecoach road and they were reining back toward the southeast and Deadhorse town.

"Curly, I brought fourteen men from the Rocking R range up here with me. They'd stay here and work in the mines—or prospect—at the drop of a hat. So would I."

She gave him a sidelong glance, and for the first time her face softened in a smile.

"If my hat hadn't washed away down the river—I'd drop it, Hal," she told him. "I—Wells Fargo could use a man like you."

He expanded his lungs with an odd exhilaration sweeping through him.

"You've hired yourself a stagecoach man, Curly," he said.

There were those in Deadhorse town who were profoundly surprised and shocked at the spectacle of Wade and Curly Joyce riding back, after so short an interval, on the lead horses of the outbound Concord. Surprise at the promptness and the unusual aspect of their homecoming;

amazement at the absence of the Wells Fargo stagecoach, and the significant presence of its treasure box on the withers of Curly Joyce's mount.

From the porch of the Blue Skull Saloon, as they rode past toward their temporary Wells Fargo headquarters in Dr. Phelps' tent, Bret Redfern and Black Bill Collier stared with surprise and shock of a different sort as the drenched riders gravely lifted their hands in mocking salute.

"Try again, Redfern!" called Hal Wade, in a low voice which hardly carried beyond the gun boss' ears. But his words reached Marshal Rocky Donovan, strolling down the board sidewalk opposite the Blue Skull dive; and he knew their import, recognized in those three words Hal Wade's challenge to the outlaw who sought to monopolize the express and mail and freight business of Deadhorse.

That night, the regular weekly issue of the Deadhorse *Observer* made its appearance from the tiny frame shack where Jimmy O'Niel kept his tiny printing press and cases of type.

Hal Wade, reading the crudely-printed frontier newspaper over his coffee and spuds and eggs in Wing Sing's restaurant just before dusk, noticed that his name was conspicuous for its absence in O'Niel's teeming obituary column.

But spread across four columns in the middle of

page one, in a box replete with typographical errors, due to the haste with which O'Niel had set up his type, was an editorial which the daring little tramp printer had set up while under the influence of righteous zeal and one too many glasses of rotgut whiskey.

The editorial referred to a news story about that morning's "accident" to the outbound Wells Fargo stagecoach, and the miraculous escape of its feminine driver and cowboy guard. It read:

> For too long, the *Observer* has been pulling its punches regarding the state of affairs in this here gold camp. Your editor has stood by and made news items out of the spectacle of innocent muckers and jack-leg engineers and mine drillers being lugged out of the Blue Skull Saloon dead and broke, when they went in alive and with gold dust enough to buck the tiger and yank out a few fistfuls of hair; if things had been run on the square.
>
> For too long the *Observer* has seen the Wells Fargo stage company badgered by its rival outfit. It has reported robberies and ambush killings without end; elsewhere in today's issue it tells of the loss of the Wells Fargo office due to fire, which fire was set deliberately, in the opinion of this newspaper.
>
> We citizens of Deadhorse have been

kow-towing long enough to the criminal element running this town. We been paying exhorbitant express rates to get our gold and silver bullion out to Carson City. We been afraid to patronize Wells Fargo, who charges standard rates. We been paying an unjust toll at the Death Canyon bridge, which was built by honest labor by all of us.

From here on out, the *Observer* ain't pulling punches or masking names. You all know who ramrods this town; you all know who's back of these killings and robberies, but you ain't had the guts to speak the name of that ramrod out loud. We can't blame you; the *Observer* has been guilty of the same hushing-up of basic facts behind these goings on.

But in the newspaper business you got a duty to perform, come hell or highwater or gun bullies. The *Observer* has been selling out, long enough. From here on out, this paper is going to show Marshal Rocky Donovan and a certain spunky woman over at the Wells Fargo office that we will back them up until Deadhorse is free of dirty skunks like BRET REDFERN and his crowd.

Yours for justice,
Jimmy O'Niel.

Wade suppressed a shudder of apprehension as he shoved back his chair, tossed Wing Sing a silver dollar, and hurried out of the restaurant.

Deadhorse was oddly quiet again, tonight; and Hal Wade, though he had only been in the Nevada gold camp a matter of thirty odd hours, knew that behind batwing saloon door and shaded dance-hall windows, other men were reading Jimmy O'Niel's sensational—and probably suicidal—editorial.

He made his way hurriedly to the little false-fronted shack where the *Observer* was published. Jimmy O'Niel, his face green-hued from the lamplight pouring through a celluloid eye-shade, was crouched over his type cases, throwing together another stick of verbal dynamite for next week's edition.

The consumptive little editor glanced up and grinned as he recognized Hal Wade entering the door and stepping past the little hand press to reach his side.

"You blew the lid off of hell with tonight's paper, O'Niel," commented the cowboy admiringly, extending a hand to grasp the printer's ink-grimy palm. I want you to know that I'm tossing my chips in the pile, backing Curly Joyce's play. I—"

Crrrrash! Glass tinkled musically from the direction of the street window, and between the words "Deadhorse" and "Observer," painted on the glass panes, appeared a tiny hole surrounded by a blossoming spiderweb of fractured glass.

Wade felt the printer's hand jerk in his own,

and turned to see a spout of brilliant crimson gushing through O'Niel's printer's apron to blend with the black ink stains there.

An ambush bullet out of the night had punctuated the editor's campaign with a ghastly, final period, before O'Niel's crusade had had a chance to gather momentum.

—Chapter IX—

WELLS FARGO DECLARES WAR

A second bullet smashed through the printing-office window, spraying Hal Wade's face with loose type from a nearby case as he tore his hand free of Jimmy O'Niel's grasp.

Dropping to a quick squat, Wade drew a six-gun and sent a single shot through the ceiling lamp overhead, to plunge the office in darkness.

As the light smashed out, Wade saw Jimmy O'Niel's legs buckle like rubber at the knees, saw type spill from the "stick" tray in his other hand.

Before the editor's collapsing body had hit the floor, the cowboy was scuttling forward toward the street door, gun cocked, thumb on hammer.

From the angle of the bullet which had nailed O'Niel and the second slug directed at his own person, Wade knew that the hidden gunman had crouched directly opposite the *Observer* office.

Squinting through the bullet-shattered window, Wade saw instantly, that there would be no chance to tally the bushwhacker.

The wide alley of a side street yawned immediately opposite; its dark recesses were crowded with ore wagons from neighbouring mines. To the right was the bulk of a livery stable; its numerous doors leading to stalls could easily have given exit to the dry-gulcher. To the left was—significantly enough—the adobe-walled structure housing Bret Redfern's notorious Blue Skull Saloon.

Wade paused, crouched at the window with wind whistling through twin bullet holes to cool his perspiring face.

Street traffic went on undisturbed; the town undoubtedly believed that the two quick, thundering shots had been the work of some drunken miner blowing off steam in a back lot.

No flicker of darting shadow appeared in the alley beyond; pedestrians moved to and fro between the *Observer* office and the blackness that held a killer.

Clamping his teeth grimly against the tragedy he had witnessed, Hal Wade made his way back between the racks of type to where Jimmy O'Niel lay groaning in his death agony.

Holstering his gun, Wade sought for and found the hand he had been clasping when the first bullet chugged into O'Niel's chest.

"Reckon this is . . . thirty . . . for me . . . cowboy," wheezed the editor, blood gurgling in his scrawny throat. "Stick by . . . that girl Curly . . . son. She's . . . thoroughbred—"

"I know that, Jimmy. I'll have Redfern's hide for this—"

"I don't . . . matter . . . son. What matters . . . is that Deadhorse is too yellow . . . to fight Redfern back . . . too cowardly . . . including me. I—"

Wade fought back a throbbing ache in his throat.

"Your last paper wasn't the work of a yellow coward, Jimmy. It'll be your monument, fellow."

In the darkness, O'Niel managed a blood-flecked grin.

"Tell Doc Phelps . . . bury me with a copy . . . of the only decent sheet . . . I ever publ—"

A ghastly rattle cut off O'Niel's words, and the shaking hand in Wade's grasp went lax.

The cowboy stood up, hitching his gun belts. Then, deciding not to take the foolish risk of walking out the front door, he left the print shop of death by a rear window and hurriedly crossed lots until he came to the Bonanza Hotel, where Curly Joyce and her father lived.

Five minutes later he had broken the grim news of O'Niel's ambush murder to the girl and Rex Joyce. Seated with them at the supper table was a bony little hombre with bright yellow whiskers, mutton chops and scanty hair on a nearly-bald pate, the fringe of hair reminding Wade of a sunflower.

"By grab, Redfern's declared open war ag'in us—an' it's up to us to fight the son—to fight to the finish!" roared the yellow-whiskered runt, leaping to his feet to shake a bony fist under Wade's nose. "Damned if I don't larrup the meat offn Redfern's bones before I'm finished with this gold diggin's—"

Wade stepped back before the fury of the little hombre's tirade, and saw Curly Joyce and her father laugh at the spectacle.

"Hal, this is our only other Wells Fargo driver, Whip Gleason," she introduced the pint-sized jehu. "You'll savvy the meaning of his Whip nickname when you see him in action. He can flick a horsefly in two without touching a leader's ear, with his bullwhip."

Wade gravely shook hands with Gleason. Not a day under seventy, Gleason was every inch a fighter. He was four feet ten inches of quivering fury, and the baleful gleam in his squinted blue eyes seemed to drill Wade as if the little man had some personal grievance against the cowboy.

"I'm takin' my stage out of here in forty minutes, Wade!" rasped Gleason, without acknowledging Curly's introduction of the Arizonan. "I'm tuckered out from bringin' the mail in this evenin', but damned if Wells Fargo is goin' to ball up its schedule just because Redfern ditched our other coach this mornin'."

Wade nodded swift approval.

"I'll be ridin' shotgun guard on that coach, pardner," he promised. "And my Rocking R gold dust will be in that strong box again, like it was this morning."

Curly Joyce reseated herself at the table and glanced at her father, to see the oldster sizing up Wade with frank admiration. No doubt Rex Joyce was remembering the day when he had been as full of fire and ice as Hal Wade and Whip Gleason were in this moment, before road agents' lead had crippled him and relegated him to office work for the rest of his life.

"You boys are both tired," the girl said. "As boss of this outfit, I'm telling you to get some sleep. You can take your stage out on the regular run tomorrow morning, Whip."

Gleason turned fiery, defiant eyes on the girl.

"By grab, you heard what I said, Curly! I was married to a hell-cat of a Mex woman for forty-odd year, an' never took a dad-blasted order from her till she croaked from frustration. I ain't takin' orders from you, neither, boss or no boss. Hal Wade an' me are takin' that stage out tonight no mat—"

Gleason's outburst was cut short by the arrival of two burly, Mackinaw-coated men whom Hal Wade sized up as mining engineers or foremen at some big gold outfit farther back in the hills, judging from their air of authority and the respect with which Rex Joyce and his daughter greeted them.

"Meet our new stage guard, boys," said the girl.

"Hal Wade, this long drink of water is Paydirt Patterson, owner of the Red Eagle gold and silver outfit, up Hawkeye Creek way. This bewhiskered mucker is Ralph Neeley, who owns the Wilderness Mine this side of Alkali Sink. Between 'em they ship more bullion out of Deadhorse than the rest of the mining outfits put together."

Patterson and Neeley nodded briefly, then turned to Curly Joyce with obvious embarrassment in their manner. Patterson spoke:

"We read Jimmy's editorial in the *Observer* tonight—"

The girl dropped her eyes.

"Jimmy's already collected a dry-gulch bullet for that piece of journalism, Paydirt."

The two miners jerked erect, faces white with shock. Then Paydirt Patterson's eyes slitted ominously.

"That settles it, Curly!" he whispered. "O'Niel gave his life to start the ball rollin' against Redfern. I reckon we been shipping our metal to Carson City by way of Redfern's Thunderbolt stagecoaches long enough. Somebody's got to start patronizing Wells Fargo, if we're ever going to bust Redfern's hold on the shipping business around here. Me an' Neeley here—"

"—have decided to risk a shipment with your stagecoach!" cut in Ralph Neeley. "An' we'll pay you the same rate we been payin' Bret Redfern's outfit."

Curly Joyce shook her head.

"We'll be glad to accept your consignments," the girl told them firmly, "but at regular Wells Fargo rates."

"Which same," spoke up Whip Gleason proudly, "are about sixty percent less than Redfern's been chargin'."

Curly Joyce turned to Hal Wade, and her eyes were shining.

"This means that tonight's Boothill Express will be carrying over ten thousand dollars' worth of Red Eagle and Wilderness ingots, Hal," she said. "That would be a fat booty for Redfern's killers to pluck. It's only fair to warn you—"

Hal Wade slapped his gun holsters.

"We'll get your Boothill Express through, Curly!" promised the erstwhile cowboy. "Jimmy O'Niel's spirit will be settin' between Gleason an' me, tonight. That set-up says we can't lose!"

Patterson and Neeley exchanged glances. They sensed the electric tension in the air. They were backing Wells Fargo with their treasure. Whip Gleason and his new shotgun guard were backing that faith with their lives.

Tonight's words were no whistles in the dark to bolster each other's courage, the mine owners knew. Wells Fargo and Curly Joyce had declared war on their murder-mad opposition: a war whose finish would be written in the slam of guns and the biting tang of powder smoke and blood.

—Chapter X—

Arrows by Moonlight

Moonlight silvered the desolate crags and buttes and shadow-etched gulches of the Badluck Range as Whip Gleason tooled the southbound Wells Fargo toward Carson City.

The stars had wheeled to the midnight position in the Nevada sky; two hours had elapsed since the red-and-yellow Concord had pulled unobtrusively out of Deadhorse.

This time there had been no fanfare of shouting men, watching the coach roll toward ominous destiny, as had been the case of the morning Concord was piloted by Curly Joyce. Except for half a dozen of Wade's cowpunchers from the Rocking R trail crew, the mining camp had been taken by surprise, as regarded the departure of a Wells Fargo coach.

Hal Wade, hunkered at ease in the driver's seat alongside the peppery-tempered little driver, was glad that their departure had been more or less unnoticed. He doubted if Bret Redfern himself was aware of Wells Fargo sending a coach out so soon on the heels of the ill-fated Concord.

Inasmuch as they were carrying ten thousand

dollars' worth of golden ingots, bearing the insignia of Paydirt Patterson's Red Eagle mine and Ralph Neeley's Wilderness outfit, Wade knew this unit of the Boothill Express would be an unusually rich target for Redfern's band of looters.

As it was, they had slipped across the Death Canyon bridge in the blacked-out interval of night between sunset and moonrise. Not even the customary toll-taker was on duty at the sturdy log gate—a factor which seemed to indicate that for once, Wells Fargo had caught Redfern's saloon gang napping.

At least, this was the opinion voiced by Whip Gleason; though Wade did not share the old jehu's optimism. True, they had put twenty odd miles between them and the gold camp, without an incident of suspicious character.

But Wade, newcomer to the Washoe gold and silver country though he was, did not underestimate his enemy. Redfern was shrewd, crafty. It was not like him to miss anything that concerned Curly Joyce or her express business; and there was nothing to keep Redfern's spies from seeing the two big mine owners paying a visit to the Bonanza Hotel, where Curly Joyce had estab-lished the new office of Wells Fargo.

"I tell you, Gleason, the night's too quiet!" repeated Wade, his slitted eyes patroling the moonlighted terrain with constant vigilance as the Concord jounced on, rocking over granite waves like a storm-tossed galleon.

Whip Gleason, one foot riding the brake as he tooled the Concord around a hairpin curve, shifted his quid of tobacco to the other side of his toothless jaw and snorted:

"We're out o' Redfern's territory now, son. No need to be spooky no more. We'll hit Carson City afore daybreak, an' have this bullion turned over to the Wells Fargo bank vault."

Wade, balancing a stubby-barreled buckshot gun across his chap-clad knees, scanned each passing chokeberry thicket and sagebrush clump with piercing eyes as the Concord rattled on across an alkali-barren sink.

"Just the same, I got a hunch buzzin' its rattles back in my noggin that somethin's wrong tonight," he said. "Damned if I can explain it, Gleason, only I've had the same hunch—sixth sense, maybe—out on bedground just before a lightnin' bolt set a herd o' longhorns to stampedin'. There's danger in the air, Gleason. I can taste it in my teeth an' feel it on the hairs behind my neck."

Gleason again snorted his contempt. Too long had Gleason rubbed shoulders with danger to trust to any nonsense like hunches.

Stagecoach drivers throughout the West were a proddy lot. On board their stage they were all-powerful, like a king on a throne or a captain of a vessel at sea. They had braved the peril of ambush too often to be—

Out of nowhere came a high-pitched, twanging sound, and something thudded heavily on the hickory footboard between Whip Gleason's boots.

For an instant the bony old driver stared aghast at the quivering ashwood shaft of an Indian arrow, its flint head imbedded deep in the tough wood, its feather a tremendous blur from the force of its impact.

Then, yanking his silver-ferruled whip from its socket, Gleason half-arose from his seat.

"Injuns!" he bawled, whipping the stage team into a sharp gallop. "Piutes or Shoshones—they ain't been prowlin' for so long, I hadn't figgered on lockin' horns with 'em tonight—"

Hal Wade swiveled in the seat, double-barreled shotgun cocked, fingers ready on twin triggers.

But he saw no sign of enemy; the moon-drenched desert was empty of Indians.

He glanced at the arrow once more, calculated its angle, then swept the skyline to the north. He picked out a craggy volcanic cinder cone, not a hundred yards beyond the stage road.

Even as he located the spot from which an ambushed redskin had undoubtedly loosed the arrow, he caught sight of three feather-bonneted figures mounted on fleet gray ponies as they spurred out of a clump of dwarf mountain mahogany on the crest of the cinder cone, spurred madly down the roof-steep slope toward the speeding stagecoach.

The range was too far for a shotgun. With swift skill, the cowboy uncocked the scattergun, leaned it against Gleason's whipstock where it would be ready to hand, and snatched up the .30-30 Winchester beside him.

Levering a shell into the breech, Wade slapped stock to cheek, drew swift bead on the galloping trio of Indians, and opened fire.

His first shot was high, but in line; he saw a geyser of volcanic dust spurt as it hit the slope of the cinder cone.

He lowered aim, triggered two fast shots; swore with pleased surprise as he saw a pony go down, throwing its rider. The feathered warrior rolled a dozen yards, then lay still as a bundle of rags.

With whip cracking like gunshots, Gleason bent to the task of keeping the stagecoach on the road as the two remaining Indians reached the level ground and started rapidly gaining.

Then, from somewhere close at hand, came an ear-stunning burst of shots. The hoarse boom of a single-shot Henry rifle crashed out from a quartzite outcrop a dozen yards from the curving roadway; a Winchester .30-30 repeater started slamming out its death song from the same hideout.

One of Gleason's swing horses, hitched between leader and wheeler on the off side, reared in the traces with a piteous squeal and then slumped, dragging all four legs.

Gleason swore with berserk rage as he felt the Concord lurch, saw the team threshing madly in harness under the bogging weight of their bullet-drilled member.

"They got us stopped, Wade—we'll have to dig in an' shoot it out with them red-skinned diggers—"

Wade swung his smoking rifle toward the quartzite rock nest and triggered the rest of the shells in his magazine at the half-hidden forms of naked warriors.

He was desperately reloading from cartridges contained in a bandolier looped about his chest when the Wells Fargo stage lurched to a final stop.

A fresh flurry of bullets raked the Concord from stem to stern, tearing splintery holes in the hardwood panels and ringing off hardware.

Gleason whipped his six lines about the Jacob's Staff and grabbed up Wade's shotgun. The cowboy, his rifle silent while he refilled the magazine, saw Gleason empty both barrels of the buckshot gun at the oncoming Indian horsemen behind them.

The latter pair divided, escaping the swarm of buckshot at that range. Bows twanged in the night, and an arrow whipped the battered old sombrero from Gleason's head, sailing it out past the threshing horses.

Another roar of gunnery came from the quartzite nest, but the bullets were directed at the team. A wheeler dropped, skull drilled dead-center. One of the leaders slumped, its withers pierced through and through by a big leaden ball fired by the Henry rifle.

"We got to hightail it for some rocks, Wade!" yelled Whip Gleason, jumping to a front wheel and thence to the ground. "Fergit the strong box—them Injuns ain't after gold. They just want scalps —an' mebbe hosses."

Hal Wade, from experience with warring 'Paches in Arizona and Comanches farther east, knew the peril of remaining in the open and opposing such overwhelming Indian odds as faced them. A Western red man could hide behind a bush that would hardly cover a quail; and in the moonlight they could melt into nothingness.

Wade leaped to the ground, rifle in hand, and took out across the sage flats behind Whip Gleason.

Out from behind a juniper snag ahead of them loomed a lone Piute war chief, judging from his eagle-feathered headdress. The Indian dropped to a quick squat, aiming a clumsy rifle at Whip Gleason's chest.

Then it was that Hal Wade witnessed the most sensational bit of self-defense he had ever seen.

Without pausing to reload the shotgun he carried in his left hand, or trying to zigzag away from the Indian who was in the act of drawing a bead on him, the bony old stagecoach man drew back the snakelike whip in his right hand.

The whip lashed outward, writhing through the air with a venomous hiss.

And the squatting Indian yelled with surprise and horror as the whip wrapped itself with magical coils about the barrel of his rifle and yanked it bodily from his fingers!

Deprived of his gun, the half-naked Indian turned to run.

The uncanny whip in Gleason's hand released its grip on the rifle, shot out through space once more, and fastened itself firmly about one of the Indian's pumping ankles.

With a squall of fright the warrior sprawled on his face, jerked off his feet as neatly as Hal Wade's lasso rope would have dumped a maverick.

Then lead spattered about them like droning bees, and the Wells Fargo reinsman dived for the shelter of a nearby pile of rocks, not pausing to disengage his long whip from the fallen Indian's ankle.

At Gleason's heels sprinted Hal Wade, rifle in hand, but with no visible target to shoot at.

A high-calibered bullet raked the flesh of Wade's thigh, hurling him off his feet even as he dived for the shelter of the basalt rocks where Gleason had taken refuge.

“Hit bad, son?” wheezed the oldster, noting the flood of crimson which gleamed on the bullhide wing of Wade’s chaps.

“Just scratched. But we’re in for it, Gleason. We’re outnumbered—an’ they’ll surround us.”

Gleason nodded, his bleak eyes sweeping the moonlighted landscape. These rocks would probably be their tombstone; their only hope was to take a few Piutes with them before scalping knives finished them off.

—Chapter XI—

Shocking Discovery

Wild Piute war whoops resounded in echo about the desert as the sound of gunfire diminished.

The Indian whom Gleason's whip had halted in mid-stride lay still in death, his skull smashed to pulp, where he had collided headlong with a rock.

Wade had accounted for one of the horsemen, further back along the stage road; but they still faced shoot-out with at least half a dozen warriors in the Indian band, judging from the number of voices lifted in wild Piute war shouts.

"Might as well resign ourselves to a wipe-out, son," grunted Gleason, worrying a fresh chaw of cut plug into his cheek. "Them Piutes are hell on red wheels when they go after scalps."

The old man chuckled as he swabbed a palm over his own gleaming, hairless pate.

"They'll be sore as rattlers in dog days when they go to peal ha'r off *this* doorknob," Gleason commented. "But that ha'r of yours will look good, Wade, hangin' from a Piute chief's belt. Or mebbe his squaw's tent pole."

Wade wriggled on his stomach to the edge of the boulder nest and raked the terrain for a target.

"Thanks," he muttered dryly. "I wish they'd get it over with. This waitin' is worse than fightin'."

Twenty minutes went by, but no further sound of combat came from the Indians they knew to be on the opposite side of the stage road.

And then, far to the south, they heard the diminishing sounds of hoofbeats drumming the night air, saw a faint smudge of alkali dust rising beyond the shoulder of the cinder cone from which had come the original arrow.

"That's a Piute trick," grunted Whip Gleason, stuffing a pair of red-jacketed shells into the breech of his shotgun. "That's to bring us out into the open—"

But moments continued to glide by, with no hint of skulking warrior or moving horse.

The suspense began to tell on Wade's nerves. Sweat bedewed the faces of both men, though the night breeze across the desert wastes was chilling to the marrow.

Crawling into the open, alert to duck back if a bowstring sent a flintheaded messenger of death winging his way, Hal Wade got a clear view of the desert flat beyond them.

The Wells Fargo stagecoach remained on the road, its bullet-riddled bulk looming behind a team that was anchored to the spot by the weight of two dead fifteen-hundred-pound carcasses.

"You wait here," Wade said, rising to his feet. "In this moonlight, I can spot a Piute as quick as he can spot me. If I draw any fire, you can back my play."

The runty old jehu squatted on his haunches with shotgun ready, as Hal Wade, ducked low and, carrying his Winchester cocked for swift action, started zigzagging toward the abandoned Boothill Express.

No shot rang out; no Indian war yell broke the stillness of the Nevada night.

Making a wide circuit, darting from rock to brush clump or keeping to low gullies, Wade made a complete circle of the quartzite nest where the Indian attackers had hidden.

But they were gone. Behind a low, piñon-scrubbed knoll, the cowboy found the hoofprints of horses, the marks of moccasin-clad feet.

There was plenty to read in that sign; and good news, for it precluded the possibility of a trap.

The Indian attackers, after halting the stage and driving its crew to cover, had given up the fray and departed.

Wade scowled thoughtfully. It didn't make sense. The redskins had them outnumbered. This was desolate malpais where reinforcements in the way of passing white men would have been very unlikely.

Yet the Piutes had surrendered the field without a single scalp or stolen horse—

Wade emerged into the open and walked down to the stagecoach. As he did so, he was surprised to note that moccasin tracks led through the alkali dust toward the Concord, where two Indians had crept up to the Wells Fargo coach from the opposite side to which Wade and Gleason had been hiding.

As a result the Indians had reached the stalled coach without being seen by the bayed white men. But why had the Indians visited the stagecoach? Were they hopeful of finding helpless passengers inside the Concord? But that was unlikely. Through the open windows of the coach, and in the brilliant moonshine, it was apparent that the Concord traveled empty of human cargo.

Wade swung up the right front wheel into the boot and lifted the canvas curtain there. Then he struck a match, to inspect the compartment where mail sacks and treasure boxes were carried.

What he saw brought an oath of surprise to his lips.

"Gleason! Whip!" yelled the startled cowboy, standing upright on the stage and waving toward the basalt pile where the veteran jehu was hiding. "Those damned redskins stole our bullion—and I thought you said Injuns didn't go for *oro*!"

Gleason came bounding out of hiding, surprise stamped across his wizened features. A few moments later he was clambering atop the driver's seat himself, to confirm Wade's discovery.

"I never heard of the likes of this, Wade!" muttered the oldster, scratching his bald dome in perplexity. "Indians don't attack stagecoaches because they want gold. They don't savvy gold. Rifles, maybe, and knives. But not bullion that's locked up in strong boxes."

The two men climbed down off the coach, each silent in his own thoughts, trying to figure out the underlying motives behind the admittedly strange actions of the Piute war party. The untimely withdrawal of the Indians, for no apparent cause; their theft of the Wells Fargo treasure—it was contrary to the redskins' psychology.

Gleason and Wade unhitched the team, using the lead horses to drag away the carcasses of the slain swinger and wheeler. Then, thanks to Gleason's expert manipulation of harness, they managed to hitch the remaining four animals to the Concord.

"Might as well return to Deadhorse town," decided Gleason. "We ain't got a cargo to deliver to Carson City. This means Wells Fargo is finished, washed up. The Red Eagle an' the Wilderness mines have lost five thousand bucks' worth of bullion apiece, an' they'll never trust us ag'in. Neither will the individual muckers or small minin' syndicates."

Wade, thinking of Curly Joyce and her dogged but losing battle against Bret Redfern's express line, shook his head grimly. Loss of business would force Wells Fargo to pull out of Deadhorse, more surely than would Redfern's criminal opposition.

Before turning the team about, Gleason turned the lines over to Wade and made his way across the sage flats to where his trusty bullwhip was still wrapped about the ankle of the Indian he had disarmed and then hurled to his death.

A startled yowl from the old man made Hal Wade freeze with alarm and leap to his feet, rifle ready to open fire on whatever enemy had surprised Whip Gleason.

But the stage driver had seen no ambushed foe, had tripped no hidden trap.

Gleason was standing in pop-eyed amazement above the corpse of the broken-skulled killer out on the moonlighted flats, even as his hands disengaged the coils of his whiplash from the dead man's foot.

"Wade! Set the brake an' rattle your hocks over here. I got somethin' to show you that'll make your eyeballs bug out!"

Scowling with wonderment, Hal Wade wrapped the lines about the coach's Jacob's Staff, locked the brake in position to prevent the four-horse span from running away with the stagecoach, and climbed down to the ground.

He hurried across the sagebrush flat to stand beside Gleason. He stared down at the dead man, who was naked from the chest up, his legs encased in fringed buckskin trousers of obvious Indian manufacture.

Beaded moccasins were on the dead man's

feet; a tomahawk hung with human scalps dangled from the corpse's belt.

Dyed eagle feathers jutted from the Indian's war bonnet. The moonlight picked out white and ochre war paint daubed on the corpse's forearms, gleaming in contrast to the coppery flesh.

"What's rowelin' you, Gleason?" demanded the cowboy. "You know this Piute?"

Whip Gleason spat a jet of amber tobacco juice at the corpse and began rolling it over on its back with his boot toe.

"Piute, hell!" snarled the oldster. "Take a look at that face, Wade!"

The Arizonan squatted down, peering at the death-contorted visage of their slain foe.

Blood had pooled and clotted over the ground in which the Indian's battered face had lain.

And then, on closer scrutiny, Hal Wade knew what had caused Gleason's excitement.

This was not the face of a Piute chieftain.

It was the leering, whisker-stubbled face of a renegade white!

Wade looked up, questioning Whip Gleason with his eyes.

The old jehu poked the corpse with a boot and snarled out:

"This ain't no Injun. It's a half-breed named Pedro Merrick—and he was a swamper in Bret Redfern's saloon in Deadhorse!"

—Chapter XII—

"Redfern'll Swing for This!"

The riddle was solved. Stray pieces of the jigsaw puzzle dropped into place, and Hal Wade saw the story of the night's stagecoach attack as a complete whole.

"I get it," he muttered, eyes meeting the sightless stare of the Indian-disguised saloon swamper. "Redfern *did* keep tabs on us, knew we had that Red Eagle and Wilderness bullion on the stage tonight. He let us sashay across his toll bridge on purpose—"

Whip Gleason nodded, running the reptilian coils of his long whip through a calloused hand.

"Of course. He disguised a gang of his Deadhorse hoodlums to look like Piutes—an' made sure we seen their war bonnets an' arrows an' heard their war whoops."

Gleason indicated the dead man at their feet with another prodding boot toe.

"They didn't figger on us tallyin' one of their raiders, where they couldn't make off with the body without gettin' some more men potted by us. All they was after was that bullion."

Wade shuddered involuntarily as he contemplated the craft and guile behind Redfern's attack. Perhaps he and Gleason had been deliberately spared, to return to Deadhorse with the information that roving Indian scalpers had attacked them, made away with the bullion which they had left unprotected on the stagecoach.

Such an admission would shatter whatever faith Paydirt Patterson and Ralph Neeley and other miners had in the ebbing strength of Wells Fargo. It would be the final blow for Curly Joyce and her hopes and dreams. Public opinion would destroy her, where Redfern could not.

"Gleason, we got Redfern where we want him, now!" exclaimed the cowboy, giving voice to his trend of thought. "We'll take this corpse back to Rocky Donovan. The marshal will identify it as one of Redfern's swampers. It'll implicate Redfern, make some of his confederates squeal to save their own mangy hides. Gleason, thanks to that wizard's whip of yours, you're going to save Curly Joyce—and Redfern'll swing for this to boot!"

With hearts suddenly exultant, the two men picked up Pedro Merrick's corpse by knees and elbows and carried it back to the stage, depositing the corpse on the floor inside between the two upholstered seats.

That done, they wheeled the Concord and set back toward Deadhorse. They had little fear of another attack from Redfern's owl-hooters disguised as raiding Piutes. Once they had obtained the gold-laden strong box they would no doubt return at once to report the success of their raid to Bret Redfern.

A quarter of a mile from the scene of the shoot-out, they made another discovery. The corpse of the Indian—or supposed Indian—whom Wade had shot at the outset of the chase was no longer sprawled in the shadow of the volcanic cinder cone.

There were tracks to show where Redfern's raiders had picked up the corpse of their fallen henchman, no doubt burying him in some out-of-the-way draw where buzzards and coyotes could not betray his grave.

"Redfern'll prob'ly send some men back to pick up Merrick's carcass," mused Whip Gleason triumphantly. "They'll figger we'll git out of this country as quick as possible, an' not take time to look over a half-naked dead man. But for once, Wade, we've outthunk that Redfern skunk—for once."

Back through the twisting climb of the Badluck grade the returning Wells Fargo Express coach toiled its way, as the moon settled behind the notched crest of a western ridge. And soon dawn began to daub the eastern horizon with vermilion.

The sun had not yet lifted when they rattled their

coach across the Death Canyon bridge and drew to a halt in front of the Bonanza Hotel.

"I'll wake up Curly an' her father," panted Gleason, swinging down from his lofty perch and tying the team to a hitch rack. "You rustle over to the marshal's shack next to Doc Phelps' tent, Wade. We'll have Bret Redfern in the calaboose before sun-up."

Wade hurried down the deserted street of the gold camp and a few moments later was rousing a sleepy-eyed marshal from the bed which he had dropped into, weary from a night's activity around the saloons and gambling dives.

As Rocky Donovan dragged on his boots and buckled six-gun belts about his massive girth, he listened intently to Hal Wade's terse description of the fake Indian attack on the Boothill Express and their subsequent discovery that one of the raiders had been a saloon bum from Bret Redfern's establishment.

"This'll give me an excuse to slap Redfern behind bars, anyhow," panted Donovan, pulling on his shirt. "It's a chance I been hopin' an' prayin' would come before a bushwhacker's slug catches me where the suspenders cross, Wade."

They hurried out from Donovan's shack to find Curly Joyce, sleepy-eyed but wide awake and grinning with excitement, just emerging from the Bonanza Hotel.

With the girl was Whip Gleason and old man

Joyce, the latter's face beaming with exultation as he listened to Gleason's news.

"I'll rustle up Bret Redfern an' confront him with one of his men disguised as an Injun," said the lawman briskly, heading for the Blue Skull Saloon. "After Redfern's in jail on suspicion, I'll search his saloon for that missin' bullion. Whether I find it or not, I'll be able to make some of his gunnies talk. We'll tell 'em Pedro Merrick did some confessin' before he died—"

Wade grinned with excitement as he followed Donovan into the sawdust-floored barroom of the Blue Skull. To his surprise, he saw that a poker game was still running full blast in one lamp-lighted corner of the big establishment.

Bret Redfern himself was dealing; the other players were coarse-voiced miners and prospectors, most of them drunk. Wade observed that the bulk of the chips were on Redfern's side of the table.

Redfern exposed his diamond-set teeth in a mechanical smile of greeting as Donovan strode up to his table. No hint of surprise was betrayed in the gambler's facial expression as he let his gaze swing over to confront Hal Wade.

"If you boys figure on setting in, you're an hour late," purred the gambler, shuffling cards with deft ease. "I'm closing up soon as this deal's finished."

Donovan's lips clamped in a mirthless smile

as he put a viselike hand on Redfern's shoulder.

"I got business with you that won't wait, Bret," he said. "Want you to come out on the street an' identify a feller that Whip Gleason brought back to town in the Wells Fargo stage."

Redfern turned his place at the game over to a house croupier and slid back his chair with negligent ease. With supreme self-confidence, the gun boss of Deadhorse adjusted his black frock coat about his massive shoulders as he followed Donovan and Wade out of the barroom's stuffy atmosphere to the cold, bracing mountain air.

"I can't see where I'd be interested in any of the Wells Fargo outfit's passengers," Bret Redfern yawned. "But anything to oblige the law, eh Donovan?"

Curly Joyce, her father and Whip Gleason left the Bonanza Hotel porch as they saw the marshal and Wade bringing Bret Redfern toward the tied-up stagecoach. The gray night was rapidly being dispelled by daylight as they halted alongside the Concord.

"By the way," grunted the marshal casually, "you got a swamper on your Blue Skull payroll name of Merrick, ain't you?"

Redfern nodded.

"That shiftless 'breed? I ain't seen hide nor hair of him for a week now. He got drunk and started pestering customers, so I fired him. Why? He got himself tangled up with the law lately?"

Donovan smiled cryptically as he took hold of the stagecoach door handle.

"Merrick," said the marshal ominously, "did a heap of talking over on Bakeoven Desert tonight, before we brought him in—"

Hal Wade, watching Redfern's face sharply, saw no muscle flinch or other outward sign that the lawman's bluff had registered with the suave saloon owner.

"You mean Merrick's in that stage?"

Marshal Rocky Donovan opened the door wide, then stepped back dramatically as he revealed the coppery-skinned, eagle-feathered corpse huddled between the seats.

Curly Joyce looked away with a shudder as Redfern leaned down to look at the dead man, then glanced up at the Indian arrow still imbedded in the footboard.

"Hm-m-m," he mused with forced interest in his voice. "Seems like old times again, Piutes jumpin' a stagecoach. No wonder folks call Wells Fargo the Boothill Express, eh, Miss Joyce?"

Donovan reached in his pocket and withdrew a pair of handcuffs. He shot a triumphant glance at Hal Wade, who waited tensely in anticipation of the surprise which would break like a tornado over Redfern's head in the next moment.

"Like hell it was Injuns, Redfern." Donovan's voice was steely. "It was a gang of your hoodlums, dressed up like Piutes. Pedro Merrick here, said plenty—before he kicked off."

Redfern grinned almost good-naturedly as he pointed at the corpse.

"If that's Pedro Merrick," he said casually, "he's sure as hell done a good job at disguisin' himself as an Injun."

Something in Redfern's tone made Rocky Donovan pause, in the act of seizing Redfern's wrist and notching his manacles thereon.

Dawn light flooded the dark interior of the stagecoach, and Rocky Donovan's face suddenly went ash-gray as he stared closer at the dead body inside.

"Somebody's loco," panted the marshal, his eyes turned accusingly at Hal Wade.

Hal Wade shouldered past the saloon owner to stare closer at the dead man. He was aware of Redfern's leering gaze as he made a discovery that left him limp with shock.

For the corpse in the stage was not that of Pedro Merrick, the disguised half-breed.

It was the corpse of a real Piute warrior, his forehead neatly drilled by a rifle bullet!

—Chapter XIII—

Kidnaped Evidence

It was fantastic, impossible. Yet it was true. The Indian who lay stiffening in death before them was not the half-breed whom Hal Wade and Whip Gleason had loaded aboard the stagecoach and brought to Deadhorse!

Wade stepped back with jaw hanging slack in amazement as Whip Gleason peered into the Concord doorway and then looked at the scowling marshal.

"I . . . I thought we had an ace in the hole, but it turned out we had a deuce, marshal," stammered the stage driver lamely. "I can't no way figure this play, but our . . . our evidence has been kidnaped, I guess."

Bret Redfern, turning up his coat collar against the chill of the mountain morning, glanced at Hal Wade with no whit of scorn or triumph in his eyes.

"What was it you wanted to see me about, marshal?" inquired the gun boss of the mining camp casually. "If it's to identify that carcass as my ex-swamper, Pedro, I'm afraid I'll have to renege."

Moving jerkily as a puppet, Rocky Donovan shoved his handcuffs back in a pocket of his Levi's. He brought himself out of his stunned trance with an effort, and snapped out:

" '*Sta nada*, Redfern. I'm through with you. For the time bein'."

Redfern lifted his sombrero in mock gallantry and made his way back to the Blue Skull Saloon.

After the green slatted doors had fanned shut on the outlaw, Curly Joyce stepped up to Hal Wade and clutched his sleeve.

"What's it all about, Hal?" she asked anxiously. "What kind of skullduggery did Redfern put over on us, anyway?"

Wade grinned ruefully as he shook himself out of reverie.

"Simple enough to figure out, but it don't put a noose around Bret Redfern's neck," replied the cowboy. "We sure as hell carried Pedro Merrick's body with us as far as here. But while Whip was wakin' you and your father at the hotel, and I was rustling up Donovan here, Redfern's men switched bodies on us."

The marshal scratched his head in bewilderment.

"What you mean, switched bodies?"

Wade pointed at the dead Indian.

"I got a strong hunch this is the Piute I bagged with my rifle when we were first attacked. They lugged his corpse back here ahead of us and were waitin' for us to show up. They knew they'd have a chance to make the switch before we could wake you up. We didn't think to guard the body—"

Donovan swore under his breath, staring at the muddled bootprints in the dust about the stagecoach. There would be no proving that Redfern's men—perhaps the very men who had been nonchalantly playing poker in the Blue Skull—had spirited Pedro Merrick's body out of the Wells Fargo stagecoach and substituted a dead Indian in its place.

"Anyhow, Redfern raked in this pot," grunted Whip Gleason, too shocked to fly into his usual rage. "We had the evidence that Redfern was behind that raid, but now all we've got is evidence that we were really attacked by Piutes."

Rocky Donovan glanced toward the Blue Skull Saloon and shrugged hopelessly.

"Wouldn't do any good to search Redfern's place and try and find Pedro Merrick's carcass," he grunted. "By now it's prob'ly bein' toted on horseback somewhere out in the gulches by some of Redfern's crew."

Wade nodded soberly.

"And you haven't any call to search his safe—if he'd be foolish enough to put that Red Eagle and Wilderness bullion in his own safe," Wade pointed out. "This Injun here blows our scheme sky-high. Even if Merrick *had* talked before he croaked, we'd never be able to make it stick in court."

Curly Joyce drew in a deep breath and slammed the stage door shut on its grisly cargo.

"Sometimes," the girl said heavily, "I feel as if the whole bunch of us haven't as many brains in our heads as Bret Redfern has in his little finger. We get checkmated on every turn—"

Whip Gleason climbed back aboard the Concord and swore lustily, the first time he had ever employed his vivid profanity in the girl's presence.

"It ain't lettin' Redfern switch dead men on us that galls me," snarled the driver, swinging the four-horse team away from the hitch rail. "It means Wells Fargo's ruined. We'll never haul another cent's worth of express or freight after news of this gets around."

Hal Wade caught the rear boot step of the Concord as Gleason headed it toward the livery-barn shed. Rocky Donovan, chin slumped on chest, headed back for his shack while Curly Joyce and her father returned to the Bonanza Hotel with heavy hearts.

After Wade had helped Gleason unharness the team and turn the horses over to a sleepy *mozo* at the livery barn, he gripped the old driver's arm.

"Listen, Whip," he said. "Redfern ain't got us licked yet, even if he has tied Donovan's hands."

Gleason eyed his young shotgun guard quizzically.

"You got a scheme brewin' in your noggin, son," the old-timer said cannily. "What's the lay?"

"When does Redfern send his next Thunderbolt Express coach to Carson City?"

"Tuesday mornin'. That's day after tomorrow."

"*Bueno.* What's to prevent us from fightin' fire with fire, Whip?"

Gleason tugged at his sunflower whiskers thoughtfully.

"Let me see if I follow you correct, son," the oldster countered. "You mean, if Redfern sticks up Wells Fargo stages, why can't we stick up one of his?"

"Exactly."

"That'd make owl-hooters out of us."

Wade hitched his gun belts excitedly as an idea took root in his brain.

"Rocky Donovan's stuck inside the law, and he hasn't made a dent on Redfern. The only reason the marshal stays alive is because Redfern's toying with him like a tabby cat toys with a mouse. The only way to buck Redfern is with brains an' bullets, Whip. We got both, ain't we?"

Gleason pondered this, then shook his head dubiously.

"I'd say yes in a second, Wade, if I thought it'd work. But suppose we stuck up a Thunderbolt stage? What would our swag be? It'd be gold dust belongin' to honest miners. Redfern don't guarantee delivery to Carson City banks; miners ship gold out at their own risk, savvy? We'd be playin' a dirty owl-hoot trick against decent men like Patterson an' Neeley."

Wade's eyes flashed with inner excitement.

"I grant you that, Whip. But that's what I'm drivin' at. Supposing we held up a Redfern stage-coach. Supposing our loot turned out to be bullion—that was stamped with Patterson's Red Eagle brand?"

Gleason paused in the act of paring a sliver of cut plug from his slab of tobacco. His rheumy old eyes flashed like a war horse hearing a bugle and shot a bony fist into Wade's ribs.

"Cowboy, you've hit on somethin' there; damned if you ain't. We'll yank a few tail feathers out of Bret Redfern, even if we have to turn outlaw to do it!"

—Chapter XIV—

Redfern's Express

On Monday afternoon, the day prior to the scheduled departure of Bret Redfern's weekly stagecoach for Carson City, Wade and old Whip Gleason departed on horseback, ostensibly on a trip to Carson City to buy another Concord to replace the one which had been totally wrecked in the Death River gorge.

Lashed to Wade's saddle, however, was a strange device for a cowboy to be carrying: a four-foot crosscut saw. And packed in his *alforja* bags, besides supplies for an overnight camp, were several sticks of dynamite with percussion caps and fuses.

Wade did not confide the purpose of these articles, even to Whip Gleason, except to say they were necessary to his "scheme."

Under cover of the night, they doubled back to the crest of Pancake Hill, overlooking the mining camp, and hid themselves in dense chaparral to await the dawn.

Shortly after sunrise, Wade was scanning the main street of Deadhorse down with his field glasses when he saw Redfern's express stage pause briefly in front of the Blue Skull Saloon to take on freight and its guards.

"He's takin' a mud wagon instead of a regular stagecoach," chuckled Wade, focusing the glasses with a thumb. "That's *bueno*—right in line with my plans, Gleason."

This morning's Thunderbolt Express was an oak-ribbed "mud wagon" of a type familiar on the overland trails where pioneers were often called upon to cross rivers without bridges or fords.

Mud wagons were built with very large wheels; their boxes were calked to prevent leakage, so that when their teams brought them down a steep bank of a prairie river and hauled them far out into "swimming water" too deep for the wheels, the wagons themselves became virtual barges. They were, literally, boats with flat bottoms and iron-tired running gear for land travel.

Painted in vivid scarlet across the box, clearly discernible in Hal Wade's glasses, were the words "Thunderbolt Express"—Deadhorse to Carson City and California—Bret Redfern, Owner.

"How many guards are ridin' with her this mornin', Hal?" panted Gleason excitedly.

Wade counted the group of horses which gun-toting men were mounting outside of Redfern's saloon. The beefy figure of Redfern himself was visible, moving around the mud wagon, giving orders to the driver.

“Jumpin’ Jehoshaphat!” exclaimed Wade. “Twelve riders, all packin’ shotguns and rifles in their boots. To say nothing of short guns in their belts.”

The old jehu at Wade’s side groaned with despair.

“That cashes in our chips before we can place a single bet,” Gleason said. “Even from ambush, Hal, we can’t buck a dozen of Redfern’s gun slammers—to say nothin’ of the driver, Scorchy Langlie. Scorchy’d be a tough customer to buck hisself. There’s only one stage driver in Nevada that’s as tough as Scorchy, an’ that’s yours truly.”

Wade lowered the binoculars and handed them to Gleason, who watched with sinking heart as he saw the Thunderbolt Express move out across the Death Canyon toll bridge, Redfern waving them good luck as they started.

Ahead of the stage rode six of the armed guards. Immediately behind it rode six others. The convoy of sharpshooters would encircle Redfern’s express wagon out in the Badlucks, making attack practi-cally suicidal to attempt.

“Listen, Gleason,” said Wade. “It ain’t normal for Redfern to put a young army like that to guard one of his stagecoaches. That means he’s carrying a gold shipment, don’t it?”

Gleason nodded gloomily.

“And more than likely,” went on Wade, “that mud wagon will be carryin’ the very bullion that his men, disguised as Injuns, choused off of our Wells Fargo wagon—bullion that Redfern'll be salting away in a Carson City bank vault. You think so?"

Gleason, watching the outbound Thunderbolt Express move in a cloud of dust up the steep mountainside below, nodded assent.

"That heavy guard means gold—*bueno*. It also means our harebrained stunt of holding up Redfern's stage is washed up."

Wade got to his feet and scuttled back through the chaparral to where their horses awaited them.

When he was joined by Gleason, Wade pointed to the big crosscut saw which he had mysteriously insisted on renting from a miner the day before.

"That saw is goin' to beat Redfern, in spite of his guard," announced Wade confidentially. "You know the trestle where the Carson City road crosses Death River at the foothills?"

Gleason nodded sourly as he tightened the latigo of his bronc's rig and scrambled into saddle.

"Yeah—I've crossed it as many times as there's hairs in my beard," grunted the oldster as they spurred out of the brush and dipped into the ravine beyond. "But what's that got to do with you totin' a four-foot crosscut saw with you?"

Wade grinned. He enjoyed rousing the old man's curiosity.

"I'm glad Redfern's shipping his express out on a mud wagon, that's all," grinned the cowboy. "Come on—we can reach that bridge in a couple of hours. But the Thunderbolt Express an' its army won't git there until noon, if then."

Gleason knew better than to press Wade for further information. Up until this time he hadn't the slightest idea why Wade had insisted on bringing a crosscut saw along with them. What connection it had with their proposed scheme to outwit Bret Redfern, Gleason did not even now fathom.

He was to find out, an hour and forty-five minutes later. Their horses were lathered by the hot, grueling trek across the Badluck ridges, avoiding the outlying gold camps and keeping out of gulches where lone prospectors might spot them.

The sun was boiling the sweat from the bodies of riders and mounts by the time they reached the stagecoach road, a good hour in advance of the time that Redfern's express coach and its heavy armed convoy would reach the same spot.

A quarter mile beyond, the road crossed Death River at a point where the river's canyon was a scant twenty feet across and less than fifteen feet from the bottom of a low trestle over the gliding water.

"We got to move fast, pardner," chuckled Wade, unstrapping the saw from his saddle and removing the heavy gunnysacks which sheathed it. “Just work, and don’t ask questions.”

Dismounting, the two men slid down the steep bank of the river to a point halfway down the length of the sturdy six-inch pilings which supported the trestle.

Horizontal logs were bolted to the upright pilings and afforded a walkway by which the two conspirators could cross the bridge below the level of the roadway.

“Here’s the lay,” explained the cowboy. “We’ll saw all eight of the timbers which support the left-hand, or downstream side of this trestle—saw ’em till they’re nearly cut through, but not quite. The cross braces we’ll saw clean through, but the cuts won’t show to anyone riding up from above.”

A gleam of understanding kindled in Whip Gleason’s eyes as he took one handle of the crosscut saw while Wade took the other.

Then, hanging onto the pilings with one arm while their feet were braced on the horizontal log, the men from Wells Fargo began sawing on the first trestle leg.

Sharp-whetted steel teeth bit into the pine log. Sawdust flew, drifting down into the swift current of Death River, which wound its way between precipitous banks as it cut through a nearby ridge.

When the first pile was sawed nearly in two, they shifted positions and set to work on the next "leg" of the small, low bridge. Averaging five minutes to the log, they had completed the job of weakening the left side of the bridge within an hour.

Then it was easier work to saw through the bracing logs which tied one side of the bridge to the other.

Work completed, the two climbed up the opposite bank, crossed the trestle on foot and paused to survey their handiwork.

There was no visible evidence to show that the Death River trestle had been tampered with. The saw cuts were out of sight to anyone approaching the bridge from either angle of the road.

Sawdust itself, grim evidence of their work, had been swept away by the muddy river below.

"It'll take at least a couple of tons to bust that bridge down," chuckled Hal Wade. "And I figger that big mud wagon loaded with freight and bullion will just about weigh two tons."

They cached the telltale saw in a scrubby thicket and remounted their horses.

Then the two Wells Fargo men scaled the southern ridge, rode a mile downstream, and hobbled their horses in a dense jungle of dwarf cottonwood and elder trees where Death River thinned out over a ford.

That done, Wade and Gleason inspected their six-guns and made their way back along the rimrock until they reached a point from which they could see the stagecoach bridge, but not be seen for intervening brush and boulders.

They did not have long to wait. Rounding a distant curve of the Deadhorse road came Redfern's stage wagon, flanked on all four sides by the heavy cordon of armed riders.

It took the better part of twenty minutes for the heavily loaded mud wagon to make its way down the twisting switchbacks of the Badluck foothills and reach the level roadway approaching the sturdy log trestle.

The two ambushers punched each other in glee as they saw the mud wagon approach the east end of the trestle. The bridge was barely wide enough to permit a stagecoach to cross; there would be no chance for Redfern's rifle-armed guards to flank the mud wagon as it crossed the bridge.

While they watched, they saw Scorchy Langlie, the veteran tooler of the mud wagon, yell orders at his guards. Six of the horsemen spurred ahead of the stage and crossed the bridge in single file, drawing rein on the opposite side to wait for the wagon and its six-horse span to cross behind them.

In the rear of the wagon the remaining six guards reined up to let Scorchy Langlie tool the heavy mud wagon across the narrow trestle.

Wade instinctively held his breath as he and Gleason crouched in their brushy ambush, eyes glued on the Thunderbolt Express.

Unsuspecting of danger, Langlie cracked his bullwhip and sent his six lathered horses out on the bridge.

Sawed-through timbers creaked and splintered under the increasing burden; but driver and guards did not hear the warning sounds above the rumble of heavy wheels on the planked trestle.

Then the mud wagon itself was rumbling out over the low bridge, and the rear guards were beginning to move forward to follow the wagon across Death River.

With a sudden crash of sound the trestle tilted to the southward, as if on a hinge.

The sawed pilings snapped like matches; Scorchy Langlie reared up in his capsizing wagon as he felt the entire trestle give way.

With a bawl of fear the Thunderbolt driver leaped for his life, his yell sounding above the frantic trumpeting of his team as the horses began skidding on the sloping top of the bridge.

Then, with a resounding splash, the wagon and its threshing team spilled over the edge to strike the swishing current below.

Spray rose in blinding sheets as the boatlike mud wagon hit Death River with a smack of sound and the sturdy-looking bridge tumbled into the river in a tangle of broken timbers.

—Chapter XV—

Gunplay and Dynamite

Too stunned by what was taking place before their eyes to move, the twelve guards hired by Bret Redfern to pilot the treasure express to Carson City sat their saddles in dumfounded amazement, eyes swiveling from the spectacle of Scorchy Langlie clinging to the wrecked bridge, and back to the Thunderbolt Express wagon which was floating shiplike down the river.

And then, from out of scrubby chaparral bordering the steep banks of Death River, appeared two figures, instantly recognizable.

"It's ol' Whip Gleason—and that salty rannihan from Arizona!" yelled one of the guards, whipping a .30-30 from his saddle boot. "Damn it—that means this bridge collapsin' wasn't an accident—"

Hal Wade and Whip Gleason were making the most of the dazed interval which followed the collapse of the trestle.

Rushing to the rimrock overlooking the river, they waited until the drifting mud wagon, with its swimming team, were immediately beneath them.

A shot crashed deafeningly from a mounted guard's rifle and a bullet cut the air inches from

Hal Wade's head as he spread his arms for balance and leaped out into space.

A five-foot drop and he landed on all fours atop the canvas roof of the mud wagon.

An instant later old Whip Gleason landed on the curved canvas hood beside him, one leg ripping a long hole in the sturdy fabric.

"Quick—inside!" yelled Wade, snatching a bowie knife from his belt sheath and making a long slash in the canvas bonnet of the wagon. "Once out of sight, they won't have anything to be firin' at—"

The yelling guards started spurring in pursuit, six of them on the west bank, the remaining six on the east bank of Death River. Scorchy Langlie, yelling profanity in the manner which had given him his pungent nickname, was crawling perilously along the upper rim of the destroyed bridge to gain the safety of firm ground.

But before the galloping cavalcade of horsemen could overtake the drifting stagecoach in the grip of the river's racing current, Hal Wade and Whip Gleason had dropped out of sight into the interior of the mud wagon via the holes they had slashed in the canvas roof.

Once inside, both men immediately knew what to do.

Scrambling over boxes of freight piled high in the mud wagon's box, they scurried in opposite directions, Hal Wade to the puckered window in the rope-laced canvas curtain in the back, and Whip Gleason up to the driver's seat recently vacated by Scorchy Langlie.

Gleason leaned far over the footboard to seize the trailing reins so as to help the swimming team.

Wade, in the meantime, had secreted himself behind the end gate of the mud wagon and thrust his rifle barrel through the oval-shaped opening in the rear of the Thunderbolt Express.

Thirty-foot cliffs were on either side of Death River and, peering upward, Wade caught a glimpse of angry-faced riders pounding along the rimrocks, hunting for a position which would give them a clear view of the stagecoach they had been paid to guard.

Gunfire hammered out viciously, and the canvas roof of the mud wagon was riddled with slugs which let in slanting pencils of sunlight.

Wade, crouched amid boxes and bales of freight and bundles of hides, triggered several fast shots dangerously close to the riders and was rewarded by seeing them spur to right and left and out of sight beyond the rim of the cliff tops.

The mud wagon, floating triumphantly as a barge, was threatening to overtake the madly swimming horses as the current increased in speed, funneling into the rapidly narrowing outlet between the cliffs.

The course of the river curved, shutting from Wade's view any sight of the trestle they had destroyed, or the infuriated figure of Scorchy Langlie.

The twelve riders hired by Redfern to guard the outbound Thunderbolt Express were having tough going, too.

It was impossible to follow the rimrocks on either bank of the river, for sheer outcrops and tangles of brush and heavy boulders flung up barriers against their horses.

Soon the disgruntled guards had dropped far behind, no longer able to catch a glimpse of the stage which was being carried at twenty miles an hour down the swift torrent.

Grinning with exultation, Hal Wade laid aside his rifle and started searching for the treasure box.

Up front, Whip Gleason had climbed out on the wagon tongue and was disengaging the tug straps from single trees to free the swimming team.

Hurling bundles right and left, Wade had little difficulty in finding Bret Redfern's iron-bound treasure box. It was padlocked, but a well-placed slug from Wade's .45 Peacemaker made short work of the lock.

For added protection against robbery, Redfern's blacksmith had bolted the gold box to the floor of the mud wagon; but Wade had no interest in stealing the chest itself.

A quick look through the box brought to light paperbound ingots of gold, most of them bearing the Lucky Lode stamp of Bret Redfern's own mine.

Pokes of gold dust, buckskin pouches heavy with treasure and sealed with their owners' names on the tag identified the gold dust as belonging to various small mines and individual prospectors.

A growing suspicion that their holdup had been in vain grew on Hal Wade as he finished inspecting the contents of Redfern's express strong box.

Then the mud wagon lurched heavily as its wheels caught on the gravelly river bottom.

Up front, Whip Gleason leaped off into knee-deep water, sloshed his way to the front of the wagon tongue and freed the horses from any connection with the grounded mud wagon.

A broad grin was on the oldster's yellow-whiskered face as he scrambled back aboard the mud wagon. Inside, he saw Hal Wade shutting the strong box and searching rapidly here and there amid the freight parcels.

"Any luck?"

Wade looked up, swabbing perspiration from his face with the sleeve of his orange-colored shirt.

"So far, no. All the ingots in Redfern's box belong to him or to other outfits he's expressin' for."

Gleason glanced apprehensively about. The mud wagon had drifted over a mile downstream and was now stranded on the shallow ford within a dozen yards of the clump of elder trees and willowbrake and cottonwoods where he and Wade had cached their saddle ponies.

Thus far Wade's experiment had worked perfectly. They had captured the Thunderbolt Express without having to fire a killing shot. The wagon itself had drifted downriver to the exact spot where Wade had figured it would drift before touching bottom.

But if Redfern's wagon turned out to be empty of Patterson's or Neeley's stolen ingots, the holdup would have been futile—and they would be branded as outlaws, every bit as guilty as any road agent in Bret Redfern's employ.

And then, as Wade was in the act of heaving aside a bundle of cowhides bearing Cal Bozeman's butcher-shop label—russet-colored hides undoubtedly skinned off Rocking R cattle brought to Deadhorse town the previous week by Hal Wade himself—the erstwhile cowpuncher made a discovery.

The bundle should have weighed not more than forty pounds. Yet its bulk caused Wade to grunt with effort as he sought to lift it aside and see what was beneath it.

"Oh-oh—I think we're getting somewhere, Gleason," panted the cowboy, whipping out his bowie knife once more. "You take my rifle and stand guard, just in case Redfern's men get here before we expect 'em."

Slashing at the rawhide strings which held the

innocent-appearing bundle of hides intact, Wade unrolled a single hide to expose a heavy iron box, smaller than the regulation stagecoach strong box.

Hugging the box in his arms, Wade made his way to the front of the stranded mud wagon and leaped out into knee-deep river water. The current was foaming noisily through the spokes of the Thunderbolt Express' wheels. Fifty yards downstream, at the west edge of the shallows, the six-horse stage team were busily grazing in lush grass at river's brink.

Wading ashore, the cowboy dropped the disguised strong box onto the mud and then burrowed his way into the cottonwoods until he came to his hobbled horse.

Unstrapping a saddlebag, he withdrew a stick of dynamite. Carefully—for in the past Wade had had plenty of experience with high explosives and knew that handling it was ticklish work—the cowboy fitted a percussion cap to the end of a fuse and the fuse into the stick of dynamite.

Then, returning to the river's edge, he proceeded to scrape a shallow hole in the mud.

In the bottom of the hole he placed the dynamite stick. On top of it, with the lid bottommost, he placed the heavily locked strong box.

"No time to pry open this tin can," yelled Wade, answering Gleason's unvoiced question as the old man stationed himself alongside the grounded stage, rifle in hand as he kept watch for Redfern's guards. "We'll blow it open, all the same as if we were desperadoes for sure—"

Gleason shrugged indifferently.

"After pullin' this job, we might as well git hung for a goat as a lamb!" returned the oldster laconically.

Wade hastily covered the strong box with mud and rocks until it was out of sight, save for the length of fuse protruding wormlike out of the mud.

"No sight of them skunks yet," panted Gleason, wading ashore. "But when they hear hell cut loose over this direction we'll have company soon enough—"

Wade took a match from the band of his Stetson and lighted the fuse. He had previously cut it two minutes in length; that would give them ample time to get a safe distance from the site of the blast.

Scurrying into the brush, the two men made their way to their horses and gripped bit rings, knowing the hobbled animals might attempt to bolt when the explosion came.

Dimly, from the north, they could hear men yelling, and the clatter of hoofbeats on rocky terrain.

"They'll follow the river until they locate their mud wagon," grunted Wade. "They know they'll catch plenty hell from Redfern if they don't bring back that Th—"

The cowboy's words were lost in an ear-splitting roar of sound.

From the edge of Death River, where Wade had planted the mysterious, hide-disguised strong box, there erupted a geyser of mud and pebbles to a height of fifty feet.

Rocks pounded through the screening foliage about Wade and Gleason with the whining fury of a hail of bullets.

Mud spattered the cliff walls a hundred yards upstream.

Horses snorted with terror down by the ford, then fled in a wild confusion of flying harness as the atmosphere thickened with ugly gray smoke and the sky rained mud, water and rocks.

Wade and Gleason paused only a moment to make sure their horses were securely hobbled.

Then they scurried out into the open in time to see the heavily locked iron strong box thud with a splash into the edge of the river.

They splashed out ankle-deep in the water and retrieved the box. Its heavy locks had been sprung by the blast, which had opened a yawning hole in the muddy bank. The metal walls of the strong box were twisted and bent, but its contents were intact as Gleason and Wade lifted it out of the water and scrambled back into the chaparral with their prize.

Moving with feverish haste, Wade unfastened

the damaged clasps, opened the bent lid on twisted and protesting hinges.

Whip Gleason leaned over the cowboy's shoulder, fanning aside dynamite smoke as he peered at the paper-wrapped bricklike parcels inside the box.

Wade lifted one of the bricks, found it abnormally heavy for an object of its dimensions.

He ripped off the heavy paper—to expose the bright-yellow gleam of an ingot of pure gold.

Stamped into the bar of precious metal was a spread-eagle design with the letters P. P.

Wade glanced up, triumph in his eyes as he met Gleason's excited gaze.

"Your hunch was right!" cackled the oldster. "That's the Red Eagle *oro* that them Injuns stole offn our Boothill Express the other night!"

Wade dropped the ingot belonging to Paydirt Patterson back into the box and closed the twisted lid.

Shouldering the strong box, he made his way back to their waiting horses, where Gleason assisted him in tying the strong box behind Wade's saddle cantle.

"Patterson an' Neeley will be plenty glad to hear about this," panted the cowboy, removing rawhide hobbles from his bronc's forelegs and swinging into saddle. "Come on, Gleason—we'll ride on to the bank at Carson City on horseback and pick up a new stagecoach for Curly on the way back.

—Chapter XVI—

Scorchy Langlie Reports

Later that day, Scorchy Langlie rode back to Deadhorse aboard one of the stocky horses which he had driven from the seat of the Thunderbolt Express that morning. Strung out behind him were the other five horses of the team.

Over in front of Jimmy O'Niel's newspaper office, Curly Joyce paused in her job of painting a sign on the windows:

WELLS FARGO EXPRESS CO.
New Deadhorse Office
Business as Usual

They had buried the martyred Jimmy O'Niel with simple honors that afternoon. It seemed fitting that the dead editor's newspaper office should house the Wells Fargo Co., since he had given his life to champion the express outfit's cause.

Rex Joyce came to the door and remarked:

"Wonder what happened to Scorchy? He's ridin' back without his Thunderbolt Express wagon."

His daughter paused thoughtfully, her eyes

fixed on the bullet holes in the window—grim reminder of the ambush attack which had resulted in O'Niel's murder.

"I'm wondering about it myself," the girl answered. "This is the first time anything ever happened to one of Redfern's wagons—and something obviously happened, because Scorchy wasn't due back until tomorrow."

Rex Joyce rubbed his bandaged head thoughtfully as he watched Scorchy Langlie turn over the lathered stagecoach team to one of Redfern's hostlers in front of the Blue Skull Saloon.

"Somethin' fishy up," admitted Curly's father.

"Yes," she answered. "I wonder—do you suppose—"

Joyce regarded her curiously as she broke off.

"You . . . you weren't about to say you wondered if possibly Hal Wade an' Whip Gleason had anything to do with Redfern's driver comin' home with his team an' minus his stage, was you, girl?" inquired the old stagecoach jehu.

Curly frowned, then turned back to her sign painting.

"I . . . I hope that isn't the case," she said. "Whip knows—and I'm sure Hal does, too—that I won't permit Wells Fargo to do business—the way Redfern does. But it *is* curious—"

She tried to shake off the suspicion that had dawned uneasily in her mind. After all, Wade and her faithful driver had left town the day before on a mission she had ordered herself, with money to buy a new Concord stagecoach and team for Wells Fargo.

Meanwhile, peppery-tempered old Scorchy Langlie had gone through the Blue Skull barroom and presented himself before Redfern in the latter's private office in the rear of the saloon.

Redfern, stripped to his shirt sleeves as he busied himself with his bookkeeping, eyed his driver in frank wonderment.

"How come you're back so soon?" he demanded, jerking a thick cigar from his teeth. "You ain't had time to get our express to Carson City—"

Scorchy Langlie avoided his chief's penetrating gaze.

"Your express is gettin' through, but our mud wagon won't be makin' the run again, boss, unless we take it to pieces an' carry it on muleback to the road again."

A bomb burst of smoke puffed from Redfern's nostrils as he sat erect with a jerk, stunned by Langlie's news. He shoved ledgers aside and raked the oldster with questioning eyes.

"It's no fault of mine, chief," defended Langlie. "For once the Thunderbolt Express met its match, that's all—"

Bret Redfern cut him off with an impatient oath.

"All right," he snarled. "What happened?"

Scorchy Langlie licked his lips and struggled for a way to outline his story. It was the first time in the years he had been in Redfern's pay that he had fallen down on an assignment, and the confession of that failure was bitter gall on his lips.

"Well, we lost a trick to Wells Fargo this mornin' at the Death River trestle," he blurted. "It was this way—"

Briefly and to the point, Langlie described how the Death River bridge had collapsed under the weight of their Thunderbolt Express, and how he had abandoned the wagon before it started its amazing float downstream.

"We caught a glimpse of Hal Wade and Whip Gleason hoppin' aboard our wagon before it drifted out of sight around the bend," panted Langlie, eyes glued to the floor. "It took us an hour to work our way to . . . to where we found the wagon grounded on a ford."

Redfern went white around the mouth. For the first time in his notorious career he had lost a trick in the grim game he was waging against all comers.

"Wade an' Gleason weren't in the wagon when we found it," went on Langlie. "They vamoosed. We didn't see hide nor hair of 'em again."

Redfern drummed the top of his desk with blunt-nailed fingertips.

"The strong box," he gruffed. "Did those Wells Fargo snakes make away with our express?"

Langlie shook his head.

"They busted the padlock—but nothin' was

missin' inside the strong box," he said, without expression in his voice.

Redfern relaxed, relief making his eyes gleam. Then his eyelids screwed together in dismay.

"I don't get it," snarled the gun boss of Deadhorse. "Why should Wade wreck our wagon, open our strong box—and steal nothin'?"

Langlie shifted nervously in his chair, at a loss for words under his boss' scathing barrage of questions.

"Where's the strong box now?"

"On its way to Carson City—with the guards. They divided up the *oro* in gunnysacks an' are ridin' to Carson City with it. The freight they left with the wagon."

Redfern leaned across his desk, his eyes boring into those of his veteran stage driver.

"That Red Eagle and Wilderness swag—that we fixed up to look like a bundle of hides," he snapped tensely. "Did—"

Langlie nodded, his eyes meeting Redfern's without flinching.

"That's what I was goin' to tell you, Bret. Wade and Gleason was wise to what we were carryin'. That was what they were after. We . . . we heard a blast. They must've opened that box and found Patterson's and Neeley's bullion. Leastwise, it's missin'."

Redfern sagged back in his swivel chair.

"They'll . . . they'll have trouble provin' that

we pulled off that robbery over in the desert the other night," panted Redfern at length. "They can't prove we knew what was wrapped up in that bundle of hides. But that don't help any. It means Wells Fargo turned the tables on us an' got that *oro* back."

Langlie nodded agreement.

"Knowin' Curly Joyce an' her methods, I know that she wasn't behind this mornin's play," gruffed the old jehu. "You got to get rid of that Hal Wade hombre, Bret—and pronto. If you don't, Wade's li'ble to get you first."

Redfern got to his feet and began pacing the floor, a thousand thoughts milling in his brain.

Langlie's report was more terrifying than a report of the total loss of Redfern's own gold would have been, for such a robbery would have enabled Redfern to force Rocky Donovan to place Wade under arrest.

But the fact that the Wells Fargo man had stolen only what rightfully belonged to Wells Fargo Express Co.—loot which Redfern had stolen from Curly Joyce's stagecoach the previous Sunday—complicated matters.

"You're right, Scorchy," panted Redfern at last. "Wade is fightin' fire with fire, as the sayin' goes. We've got to get Wade—before he gets us!"

—Chapter XVII—

A Receipt for Bullion

It was two days later when Wells Fargo's Boothill Express once more entered the scene.

Hal Wade and Whip Gleason returned to Deadhorse as scheduled, riding in the driver's seat of a new red-and-yellow Concord stage which they had purchased from the Pioneer Overland outfit in Carson City.

Bret Redfern was absent from town, on a visit to his Lucky Lode gold mine back in the hills. The streets were deserted, it being too early in the afternoon for the gambling halls and saloons to be open.

The new stagecoach rolled to a halt in front of Jimmy O'Niel's office, and driver and guard dismounted to receive the greetings of Curly Joyce and her father.

After the stage team, also newly purchased from a livery outfit in Carson City, had been turned over to a *mozo* from the Silver Nugget Livery Stable, the two dusty expressmen made their way into the new Wells Fargo office.

Waiting for them inside were two burly miners whom Wade recognized as Paydirt Patterson and Ralph Neeley, the mine owners.

"I'm right glad to see you boys," said Wade, reaching in a crescent-shaped pocket of his rodeo shirt and withdrawing a sheet of paper. "I brought this back for you from Carson City."

Curly Joyce was looking at Wade sharply as she saw her new stage guard hand over the paper to Paydirt Patterson. The big miner took it and frowned curiously.

Then he glanced over at Curly Joyce, and a grin dawned on his grizzled face.

"I'll be damned—beggin' your pardon, Miss Curly," exclaimed the owner of the Red Eagle Mine. "This is a receipt from my bank in Carson City sayin' that Wade deposited our missin' bullion to mine an' Neeley's accounts yesterday!"

The girl seated herself at O'Niel's desk as if unable to comprehend what Patterson had said. Then she turned her blue-eyed gaze on Hal Wade, only to see the cowboy calmly rolling a cigarette.

"All right, Hal," she said. "Suppose you let your boss in on the secret."

Wade looked at her with an expression of wounded innocence.

"What secret?"

Curly Joyce licked her lips in an effort to control her agitation.

"All right, Hal. You and Whip reported an Indian raid in which you lost our strong box with Patterson's and Neeley's gold shipment aboard.

You . . . you brought back a dead Indian to prove it, and we've duly buried the Indian."

Wade and Gleason exchanged glances.

"Oh—that!" answered Wade, lighting his quirly with a flourish. "Thanks for plantin' the Injun."

"If you lost the gold shipments," continued the girl patiently, "what is this piece of paper—this receipt—you just handed Mr. Patterson?"

Wade seated himself on a stone-topped printer's table and laced fingers about a chap-clad knee.

"That's a *bueno* receipt, Curly. Gleason an' myself deposited that gold shipment personally in the bank at Carson City yesterday. You might be interested to know that my Rocking R Syndicate's gold shipment is also now on its way to Arizona."

Curly Joyce squirmed with exasperation.

"As your employer," she snapped, "I demand to know how you recovered that lost gold. Mr. Patterson and Mr. Neeley deserve to . . . to know . . . and—"

Wade eyed the two mine owners blandly and saw them making an effort to hide their smiles.

"We ain't in the least interested in Mr. Wade's . . . er . . . methods of carrying gold shipments, Curly," countered Ralph Neeley. "The thing is, Wells Fargo carried the gold through—and we've got official bank receipts to prove it. That's all that counts with us."

The two mine owners got to their feet and made for the door. On the threshold, Paydirt

Patterson turned and lifted his hat in Curly Joyce's direction.

"Furthermore," said the owner of the Red Eagle Mine, "we will be shipping our next consignment of bullion on your Boothill Express. Adios!"

After the two miners had departed, Curly Joyce swung on Hal Wade with an exasperated cry.

"You . . . you know it isn't right to keep a woman guessing!" she stormed with mock anger. "I think I can pretty well figure things out, though. Did you . . . did you hold up Bret Redfern's Thunderbolt Express Tuesday afternoon?"

Wade and Gleason looked at each other with pretended humiliation.

"Do we look like *bandidos*?" they protested in unison.

Rex Joyce lighted his pipe and hid his own glee behind a thick curtain of smoke.

"Don't press the boys too hard for details, Curly," he advised his daughter. "Then, when Rocky Donovan asks embarrassing questions, you won't have to do any lyin'."

Hal Wade flicked ash from his butt and eyed Rex Joyce quizzically.

"Has our worthy marshal some questions to ask of Wells Fargo?" he inquired innocently.

Joyce shrugged noncommittally.

"I have serious doubts," spoke up Whip Gleason, "that Bret Redfern will be reporting anything unusual to the marshal of this here town."

Curly Joyce swung on Wade and demanded pointblank:

"Hal, tell me—did you two rapscallions recover our stolen gold shipment by waylaying Redfern's express wagon? Did you?"

Wade felt a slight surge of confusion.

"Well—yes, Curly," admitted the cowboy. "And now, Whip, what say we cross over to Wing Sing's place and get some chuck? As for you, Curly, don't ask your men too many questions. It ain't ladylike to be so curious."

With which calm dismissal of the subject, Wade and Gleason hastily vacated the Wells Fargo office and headed for the chink café.

A strange torment of emotions stirred Curly Joyce's heart as she watched the two cross the street. Rex Joyce, watching her, chuckled sagely behind his pipe smoke.

"Somethin' tells me," he remarked, "that Hal Wade's li'ble to be callin' me dad-in-law before he knows it. And you ain't exactly discouragin' his progress along that l—"

"Oh, shut up, dad!"

Curly's outburst silenced the oldster, but the flush of color in her face belied her anger.

—Chapter XVIII—

A Message from Paydirt

After night had fallen over Deadhorse town and the saloons had opened their doors to the usual throngs of tired and thirsty men from the outlying mines, Hal Wade made his way back to the new Wells Fargo office in the newspaper shop.

Whip Gleason, who could face a road agent's gun without batting an eyelash, was keeping a safe distance from Curly Joyce.

Wade was disappointed, but likewise relieved, to find Curly had locked up the office for the night.

Admitting himself by means of a key that had been given to him, Wade seated himself at the girl's desk, lighted a kerosene lamp, hooked spiked heels over the rung of his chair and started rolling a quirly.

Things were going fine, now. The recovery of the stolen gold shipment for Patterson and Neeley had put Wells Fargo back on its feet again; when news of the exploit was winded around the diggings, it would enhance the prestige of Curly Joyce's stagecoaches a hundred percent.

As he sat musing there sounded a knock at the door, the sound of the knob turning.

Hand slapping instinctively to gun butt, Wade whirled in the swivel chair, eyes slitted warily as he saw the door open to admit a bony-faced old hardrock miner in the warped boots and patched clothing of a typical mucker.

"You Hal Wade?" questioned the prospector uncertainly, eyes blinking against the lamplight.

"I'm Wade."

"Paydirt Patterson sent me down here, Wade," said the mucker. "I'm s'posed to guide you back to the Red Eagle diggin', if you can come tonight."

Excitement made Wade's heart hammer his ribs. He remembered Patterson's promise that his next shipment of gold would be routed out of Deadhorse by way of Curly Joyce's stagecoaches.

This message, sent by confidential carrier direct to him, would probably contain news of interest to Wells Fargo. Nor was Wade mistaken:

> Wade: I have called a meeting for tonight of all the small-mine owners and individual prospectors operating around Hawkeye Gulch. I expect to be able to steer all their business to Wells Fargo, once they know Curly's Boothill Express coaches are starting to get through safely. I think it will help restore their confidence if they can see and talk to you, Wade. You talk their language.
>
> If convenient for you to come up to the Red Eagle tonight and attend the meeting, do so.

There's room in our bunkshack for you to stop over tonight.

Am sending this by Sam Smith, one of my drillers. He'll guide you back to Hawkeye Gulch. You can trust him. Try and make it as this is important to Curly Joyce.

PAYDIRT PATTERSON.

Wade dropped Patterson's note on the desk, blew out the lamp and hitched up his gun belts.

"Lead the way, Smith!" he grinned, locking the office door and turning to the mine driller. "I'll pick up a horse at the Silver Nugget and be right with you."

Ten minutes later, Wade and Sam Smith were cantering out of town, heading into the rugged Badluck hills. The moon had not yet risen, but the winding trail that had been beaten smooth by the hoofs of hundreds of ore-laden mules stretched off in a zigzag ribbon to the northeastward.

"How far is it to the Red Eagle outfit, Smith?" asked the cowboy.

The driller grunted, spurring his horse alongside Wade's stirrup as they left the lights of Deadhorse behind them.

"Six mile—takes an hour to make it on hossback."

Wade's heart pounded. Getting Paydirt Patterson as an active ally was a major victory for the Boothill Express. Tonight's mass meeting of smaller miners would result in taking away hundreds of dollars' worth of business that had previously been monopolized by Bret Redfern, and Wade knew that his visit to that meeting would be of tremendous importance to Curly Joyce.

The knowledge that he could be in a position to serve Curly Joyce in a substantial manner warmed Wade as they rode onward through the night, dark hills closing in about them as the trail climbed higher into the desolate badlands.

The trail narrowed, but was plainly visible under the starlight. At one point, where it dropped steeply into the black gulf of a ravine, Sam Smith reined up and permitted Wade's horse to precede him.

"Maybe you better go ahead, Smith," suggested Wade, reining to a halt. "I never been on this trail before. My bronc can follow yours in the dark, I reckon."

The mine driller grunted assent. Invisible in the blackness, he spurred past Wade on the narrow trail.

Then something hissed through the air when Smith was abreast of Wade's stirrup.

An instant later the tight noose of a lariat dropped over Wade's hatbrim and snapped tight, closing with a strangling grip about his throat.

Too late, Wade snatched for his guns, then felt

himself being jerked bodily from saddle as Sam Smith spurred his horse violently forward.

Wade crashed to the ground in a shower of stars, his hands leaving his gun butts to claw frantically at the rawhide noose which threatened to choke the air from his lungs.

Smith dismounted, saddle leather creaking as he leaped to the ground. Then a six-gun made a scraping sound as the miner jerked it from leather, still maintaining his throttling grip on the noose which he had dropped around Wade's throat.

Faint light glinted off the barrel of Smith's Colt as it lifted and fell, the steel thudding soddenly off Hal Wade's skull.

Limp as a sack of spuds, the man from Arizona slumped in the darkness at the feet of his traitorous guide.

—Chapter XIX—

Inhuman Revenge

Whistling tunelessly, Sam Smith removed the noose from Wade's neck and struggled to hoist the unconscious man aboard his horse.

Jackknifed over the saddle, Wade sprawled limp as a dead man, head and arms dangling down one side of the horse, legs down the other.

Still whistling, Sam Smith mounted his own saddler and headed off into the ravine, trailing Wade's horse by one rein.

For a quarter of a mile, Smith led his unconscious captive into the desolation of the Badluck Range.

There the trail forked, the well-beaten path snaking off into a series of switchbacks to the mines which lined Hawkeye Creek, rich lode that had already produced more than a million dollars' worth of silver, gold and lead for its workers.

The trail to the south was overgrown with weeds, frequently wiped out by small earth slides, trackless from disuse.

Down this trail Smith headed, and soon the night had swallowed them up.

Then, out of the shadows along the trail side,

emerged sombreroed men, their eyes glittering in the faint wash of starlight.

"Got 'im, Smith?" came a gruff voice, challenging the miner.

"Yep. No trouble. Swallered our bait an' come hightailin' smack into our trap."

Wade felt himself lifted out of saddle. Rough hands jerked his arms behind his back, lashed his wrists together with rawhide pigging strings. Other hands unbuckled his shell belts and gun holsters.

Opening his eyes, Wade peered up through a curtain of swimming fireworks to stare at his captors.

A match flared as one of them lighted a cigarette, and by the weak yellow glare Wade recognized the horse-faced killer known as Black Bill Collier.

A cold chill of despair coursed through Wade's being, shocking him back to full consciousness of his situation.

Black Bill Collier—Redfern's right-hand man!

Patterson's note, then, had been forged. It had been the bait that had lured him into a mantrap, from which he knew he would never emerge alive.

Worse yet, Curly Joyce or his other friends back in Deadhorse would never know his fate. No one had seen him leave the mining camp with Smith. He had no idea how long he had been unconscious or how far he had been brought, or in what direction Smith had ridden after clubbing him to insensibility.

Brutal fingers clutched his collar, jerked him to his feet. Staring groggily about, Wade suddenly jerked erect as his eyes focused on a towering hombre standing beside Black Bill Collier.

"Redfern!" he gasped.

The flinty-eyed gun boss of Deadhorse town nodded.

"Welcome to Dead Man's Gully, Wade. You aren't the first hombre to leave his bones here for the coyotes. Only in this case the coyotes'll never find your bones—if that's any satisfaction to you."

A moon, white and oblong as the glazed eye in the face of a corpse, was slowly lifting above the craggy ridges, bathing the ravine with unearthly light.

The silvery beams picked out the harsh lines of hate and fatigue on Bret Redfern's visage. Moon rays glinted off the beads of sweat on Sam Smith's brow, off the yellow, crooked teeth under Black Bill Collier's peeled-back lips.

"Looks like you win this pot, Redfern," admitted Wade, the effort of speech making his bruised skull ache as if a hammer was striking it with each word. "But ambushin' me isn't going to put Wells Fargo out of business, if that's what you're aimin' at."

Redfern shrugged indifferently.

"Maybe not, Wade, but it'll go a hell of a long way in that direction. I'd have had Curly Joyce run out of Deadhorse by now if you hadn't come on the scene."

The killer turned to Sam Smith.

"Light the lantern, Sam!" he gruffed. "This is no time for palavering. Let's get it over with."

Sam Smith groped in the brush and brought out a kerosene lantern. He propped up the chimney, ignited the wick, and then returned to the two outlaws who stood on either side of Hal Wade.

"This way, pards," grunted Smith. "This mine tunnel only goes twenty yards into the hills, an' you can take it from me, no man livin' knows about this tunnel but me. I staked out this gulch before Old Pancake Comstock hit his silver lode in the Washoes an' put Nevada on the map. Nobody's been here before or since. There's no pay dirt to bring 'em, damn it!"

Redfern and Collier grasped Wade by the elbows and moved him forward to follow Sam Smith deeper into the pit of the brush-choked ravine.

The fitful rays of the lantern cut through the ebon shadow to illuminate the still blacker opening of a mine tunnel at the base of the north slope. It was heavily timbered, barely as high as a man's head, and not more than three feet in width. It was but one of hundreds of similar burrows made by prospectors in the honeycombed hills of the Washoe region, in search of treasure-bearing ore.

Stooping, Sam Smith entered the tunnel, pawing his way through curtaining spiderwebs. The lantern light seemed unable to make the dense blackness retreat before it.

A few yards inside the shored-up mouth of the abandoned diggings, the tunnel widened into a small chamber where Smith had gouged out in various directions with pick and shovel before giving up the lode as not profitable. No shafts or tunnels led away from it, so that it formed a rock-walled prison.

"Here's where we'll be saying adios, Wade," clipped Bret Redfern, shoving the cowboy headlong against the rock wall and lashing a brutal kick to the Arizonan's groin.

Wade gasped, partly from the pain of Redfern's kick and partly from the rage which stormed through him in a wave of desperation.

"What . . . play . . . are you ribbin' up against me, Redfern?" he panted.

Redfern's visage was a black-and-yellow devil's mask in the guttering lantern rays, the diamonds in his front teeth glittering in uncanny resemblance to a pair of eyes.

"We've got a dynamite stick planted on the uphill side above the mouth of this tunnel," answered Redfern. "When Smith touches it off, the whole hillside will spill down into this ravine."

Black Bill Collier laughed callously as he saw the color drain from their prisoner's countenance.

"You won't have to worry about your carcass being disturbed by buzzards or wolves or even worms, amigo!" jeered the lantern-jawed crook. "You'll be sealed up behind hundreds of tons of rock an' earth. This ravine's off the beaten trail, in barren country, where prospectors won't be grubbin' with picks. So your bones will be intact, all right, when Gabriel toots his trumpet."

Wade glanced desperately about him, knowing that escape was futile.

As if fearful that their prisoner would go berserk at the prospect of being entombed alive, Bret Redfern stepped in with a savage oath and brought up a knuckle-bunched fist in a smoking uppercut.

The fist caught Wade on the point of the jaw, snapping his head back.

His shoulder blades crashed heavily into the back wall of Smith's rock-hewn chamber, but he was out cold when he collapsed to a sitting position at Redfern's feet, then slowly toppled sidewise to push his cheek into the rubble.

"Come on," grunted Redfern. "Let's get out of here."

With a final glance at the man left to eternity, the three outlaws made their way outdoors again, Sam Smith bringing up the rear with his smoky lantern.

Once outside, Collier and Redfern made their way out of Dead Man's Gully to where they and their horses had awaited Smith's arrival with their captive from Deadhorse.

Smith, meanwhile, scrambled up the rocky slope above the mouth of his worked-out slope. The lantern light picked out the wirelike fuse which he had connected to a single stick of dynamite buried in the gravel earlier that day.

Smith struck a match, lighted the fuse, watched it sputter and throw off sparks.

Then, lantern swinging at his side, Smith started to scurry down into the ravine to rejoin Redfern.

Even as he did so, a rifle shot rang out and a spurt of red flame came from the spot where Redfern crouched in ambush, fifty yards away.

Without knowing what had smashed the brains from his skull, Sam Smith collapsed and rolled like a log down the slope.

"No use havin' a witness to get drunk an' give our job away," commented Redfern, thrusting his rifle in its saddle boot.

Before the murdered man's corpse had rolled to a stop in the brush below, the dynamite exploded with a blinding flash of light and a road that seemed to split open the sky.

It was not a large blast in itself, but on the heels of the explosion came a dull, earth-shaking rumble as hundreds of tons of rock and loose earth avalanched down the hillside to block the bottom of the V-shaped ravine.

Minutes later, when the rocks had quit sliding, the mouth of Sam Smith's abandoned mine was erased from sight under a mountain of earth. Only the stars knew the spot where Hal Wade had been buried alive.

—Chapter XX—

When Hope Is Dead

Consciousness returned to Hal Wade in glittering fireworks. Rockets burst in pink fury before his eyes. Bomb bursts hammered his skull with fire and numbed his ears with their steady roar.

But he opened his eyes to find that his tortured senses had been tricking him.

The stars and skyrockets were figments of a deranged optic nerve; in reality his eyes had opened upon blackness so intense that no whit of light would have been visible even if it had been high noon instead of midnight.

The sound of cannonading in his eardrums was the beat of his own heart, driving sledgehammer blows in his chest.

Gradually, as he sat up and the blood cleared from his bruised head, the fireworks began to dim. The tom-toms in his inner ear continued to throb, but not so noisily.

Memory returned with his clearing senses.

"I'm in a mine—I'm in a mine—I'm alone—"

He babbled the words, and taunting echoes rang from a dozen points to mock him, as if he were inside a barrel talking to himself like a crazy man. There was the same dull booming cadence to his words, banging back at his ears from nearby confining walls that acted like soundboards. He wondered why the rapid drumming of his heart was not picked up by echo, too.

He tugged at a hand, intending to massage his bruised jaw with his fingers to ease the pain caused by Bret Redfern's pile-driver blow to his chin.

Then he realized suddenly that his original captor, the whiskered mucker Sam Smith, had bound his arms behind his back with rawhide pigging strings.

The pain in the region of his shoulder blades was intolerable, but he knew how to correct that.

Getting to his feet the cowboy moved away from the sharp rock walls and halted in the middle of the rock-ribbed chamber.

Then squatting down he was able to draw each booted foot inside the circle of his tied wrists, thereby bringing his long arms in front of his body.

Still seated, Wade started doggedly to work on the rawhide string which lashed his arms, gnawing at the knots with his teeth.

The flesh of his wrists had swollen, puffing around the rawhide strand and cutting off the circulation in his hands.

Pain stabbed up and down his arms as he chewed at the stubborn knots which Sam Smith had tied.

After an eternity of time, the whang-leather strip

loosened and shook free. Blood tingled back into palms and fingers, as he flexed his hands.

He fumbled in his chaps pocket for matches. Like a condemned prisoner ticking off the days of life remaining to him before the gallows claimed him, Wade counted the matches.

Thirteen of them—

He struck one, peered about at the walls of his prison.

Unlike most mines, the rocks were not slick with water. Dead Man's Gully was merely an arroyo in heat-blistered desert; no seepage polished the walls or ceiling of his grave.

The guttering flare of the match showed him the pick marks where Smith had hacked out this hole in the mountainside in his futile search for pay dirt in some bygone day.

There were a few feathers and some small dried bones lying underfoot, proof that a coyote had denned here at some time or other. A faint animal odor still clung to the rocky chamber.

The match scorched Wade's fingertips, pinched out.

The darkness that rushed in on the heels of the dying match was almost tangible. Its unseen fingers seemed to flatten the hair on Wade's scalp, press against his eyes.

Stifling a mad desire to scream out in horror, the cowboy felt his way around the circle of rock walls until he found the opening.

Dust hung thick in the air of the tunnel, choking him as the rocky particles reached his nasal passages and lungs.

Then, midway out of the exit tunnel, he came up short with his boots ramming into dirt and rubble.

He scratched his second match, and got his answer for that.

"Plugged up tight. Might as well be in a coffin with six feet of clods over me."

It was true. Sam Smith's abandoned mine tunnel was a grave. Redfern had carried out the grim threat he had voiced just before his knockout punch had dropped Wade in his tracks.

The exit tunnel was jammed with earth—fresh earth, from ceiling to floor.

The atmosphere held a sinister, unseen pressure, which Wade's sensitive eardrums registered. That meant that he was buried under tons of earth. It was similar to the feeling he had experienced when deep under water, the day he and Curly Joyce had plunged to the depths of Death River.

Curly Joyce! The girl's face swam in the blackness before Wade, and brought an odd sense of comfort to him.

Then the knowledge that he would never see her again—that his eyes would never even see daylight again—made a feeling of panic well up in his heart, smothering him.

He clawed out his pocket watch, struck another match. The hands pointed to two-fifteen.

"That's probably a. m.," he mused aloud. "Means I was knocked out colder'n a mackerel for three hours, anyway."

He wound up the watch, grateful for the sound its tick made. It was like a human heart, beating along with his, keeping him company in his last hours.

Returning to the wider chamber where the air was not quite so thick with dust, Wade lay down.

Gradually his tangled thoughts dulled, and he slept.

Hours later a smothering sensation made the cowboy leap to his feet in the darkness. He was clawing at his throat, like a strangling man.

For several minutes, he had difficulty in realizing where he was. It was like awakening from a nightmare, only to find himself in the grip of an even worse nightmare.

He struck another match, looked at his watch. The hands pointed to one-thirty.

"That means—I been sleeping all through the morning, and this is afternoon," he panted. "And I'm hungry—"

The pain in his jaw had left, only to be replaced by the ravages of thirst and hunger in his empty stomach. And the smothering sensation that had roused him out of sleep—he knew well enough what that was.

The scanty oxygen supply in the cavern was

giving out. Tons of rock plugged up the door of the mine tunnel, through which air from the outside world could not filter.

Automatically he groped hands to his thighs, intending to jerk six-guns from holsters. If suicide were ever justifiable it would be in his case.

But the guns, of course, were not there. Redfern would have stripped him of weapons before plunging him into this lightless, airless cubicle to play out his string.

He picked up a smooth pebble and started sucking it, in the manner of desert-bred Indians who wished to quench their thirst on long treks through arid country. But soon even his salivary glands were dry, and he could sense that his tongue was swelling rapidly, that his lips were cracking, that the roof of his mouth was parched and blotterlike.

"No use hopin' for rescue," he groaned aloud. "Nobody knows I left Deadhorse. And Redfern's too slick to leave any clues behind."

Suddenly, as might a crazy man, Hal Wade leaped at the confining rock walls and hammered them until the pain of his battered, bleeding knuckles made him cease.

His sanity would topple before merciful death by starvation came. He found difficulty in dragging the dust-laden air into his lungs. It was dead, fetid air, sterile, foul.

Getting a grip on himself, Wade sat down. He

couldn't let himself think—couldn't go into another crazy outburst of fighting the walls that hemmed him in.

He tried to seek merciful oblivion in sleep, but his hunger-racked body would not permit sleep.

Buried alive—buried alive—the words began chanting themselves over and over again in his tortured consciousness.

Then, moving as if in a stupor, he pulled the remaining nine matches from his pocket and commenced striking them. The dark had suddenly become terrifying, and he felt that only in the feeble flicker of the matches could he find respite from the insanity that was fast overtaking him.

The matches did not glow so brightly, any more. When the thirteenth and last match was gone, Wade realized that he had doomed himself to die in darkness. Only the faint sulphurous odor of the matches remained in the air, taunting his nostrils, reminding him that his eyes had registered their last sight for all time.

With the coming of total darkness again, hope ebbed and died in Wade's heart. And when hope is gone, little remains to keep a man alive.

He was in good physical condition. He wondered how long a man could live without food or water —but death by asphyxiation would claim him before starvation did. It would be better that way.

Sometime, hours later, when the choking sensation in his lungs could not be allayed by jerking open his shirt collar, the air in the mine tunnel would be dead at last.

Consciousness left him. Inert, sweat-drenched, Hal Wade collapsed on the rock-strewn floor of his tomb, and the spark of life flickered, ebbed, rallied feebly within him, then edged off into the last faint smolder that comes before merciful death.

—Chapter XXI—

Wings of Death

The world was a happy place to live in. For the first time in the five years that Curly Joyce and her father had been in Deadhorse town, the girl awakened on a happy morning.

Setting her cream-colored Stetson at a jaunty angle on her copper curls, the boss of the Wells Fargo branch express line from Carson City to Deadhorse town made her way out of the Bonanza Hotel and swung briskly down the main street toward her new office.

Bartenders, busy sweeping off saloon porches, called greetings as Curly Joyce strode past, her high-heeled cow boots ringing briskly on the scuffed wooden sidewalks.

She answered with friendly smile or lift of hand, for she could count most of these grizzled, flint-eyed men as her friends. A lone girl waging a lone fight against bitter odds, she had the support—at least spiritually—of the vast majority of the gold camp's citizens.

The sky was flawlessly blue; the Nevada sun beamed a warm welcome on her, as she turned in at the Wells Fargo office which had, up to the time of its editor's murder, been the print shop from which the Deadhorse *Weekly Observer* had been printed.

Curly Joyce was humming a glad song as she unlocked the door of the office and seated herself at her desk.

Paydirt Patterson and Ralph Neeley would be in sometime during the day with gold dust which she would not have to ship out of town on her Boothill Express coaches. It would belong to Wells Fargo, as express fees for getting their bullion to Carson City.

At dawn that morning, she had looked from her hotel window and had seen Whip Gleason ride out of town on his new Concord, carrying the outbound mail to Carson City.

The news had gone the rounds of Deadhorse's saloons and gambling halls last night, concerning the big gold shipments which Hal Wade had taken safely to Carson City.

That would restore the gold camp's confidence in Wells Fargo. Other miners, eager to avoid paying Redfern's exorbitant express charges, would be tempted to switch their business to Wells Fargo.

"Yes, it's a grand world," the girl commented to herself, as she feasted her eyes on the black-inked entries she had made in her ledger. "It's a grand—"

She broke off, as a strange sheet of paper met

her eyes. She picked it up, and her lips moved soundlessly as she read:

> Wade: I have called a meeting for tonight of all the small-mine owners and individual prospectors operating around Hawkeye Gulch. I expect to be able to steer all their business to Wells Fargo, once they know Curly's Boothill Express coaches are starting to get through safely. I think it will help restore their confi-dence if they can see and talk to you, Wade. You talk their language.

A thrill coursed through Curly Joyce as she glanced on down at Paydirt Patterson's signature.

"Good old Paydirt," she breathed. "He's got the biggest outfit in the Washes, next to Redfern's Lucky Lode. If he backs me—"

She read on:

> If convenient for you to come up to the Red Eagle tonight and attend the meeting, do so. There's room in our bunkshack for you to stop over tonight.

Curly Joyce nodded to herself. She and her father had wondered, at breakfast, why Hal Wade hadn't showed up to eat with them. He hadn't ridden out with Whip Gleason that morning because there was no freight of value on the outbound stage which would require his presence as guard.

This note accounted for Wade's absence, then; he had simply spent the night up at the Red Eagle mine, attending Patterson's informal miners' meeting.

It did not occur to the girl to resent not having been invited to that meeting, although she was the head of the Wells Fargo outfit in Deadhorse. After all, being a woman was a handicap in running a Western stage outfit. She admitted that, freely enough. As Patterson's note had said, Wade talked the language men could understand. As her representative, Wade would get their business for Wells Fargo, if any man could.

She went on with Patterson's message:

> Am sending this by Sam Smith, one of my drillers. He'll guide you back to Hawkeye Gulch. You can trust him. Try and make it as this is important to Curly Joyce.
>
> Paydirt Patterson.

A frown gathered between the girl's brows.

"Sam Smith?" she queried. "Since when has Paydirt been hiring that drunken sot to work for him? He never did any mine drilling in his life, that I know of—"

A shadow fell through the street window and across her desk, and she looked around to see Paydirt Patterson himself opening the door.

A friendly grin on the big mine owner's face as he doffed his sombrero.

"*Buenos dias*, Curly," Patterson greeted. "Happened to be in town shoppin' for some bracing timber for a new shaft I'm sinking. Tapped a new lode yesterday."

Curly Joyce extended a hand in warm welcome to the grizzled old miner.

"Paydirt, I just happened to run across the note you sent Wade. I want to thank you for calling that miners' meeting last night—knowing you did it in my behalf. It was—wonderful of you."

A puzzled look crossed Patterson's face.

"Note to Wade. Miners' meeting?"

"Why, yes. Did you call it off?"

Patterson scratched his gray-thatched scalp.

"I didn't call no meetin', Curly."

A feeling akin to panic gripped Curly Joyce as she thrust Hal Wade's message into his hands.

"Didn't you send for Hal Wade to come up to the Red Eagle last night, Paydirt?"

The old mine boss caught the terror in Curly's voice as his eyes shuttled rapidly over the scrawled message.

"I never laid eyes on this note before, Curly. This shore ain't my handwritin'."

With a low cry of alarm, Curly Joyce leaped to her feet.

"Wade's been trapped, Paydirt. Come on. I've got to tell Rocky Donovan about this—"

They found the town marshal drinking his breakfast coffee in Wing Sing's restaurant. Donovan's eyes went bleak as he read the note bearing Patterson's forged signature.

"Looks *muy malo*," admitted Donovan tensely. "You saddle up a bronc, Curly—we got some ridin' to do. I'll hustle over to the Bonanza and see for sure if Hal Wade ain't still asleep."

The look on Rocky Donovan's face, when he returned from the ramshackle hotel, told Curly the worst before Donovan reported his findings:

"Wade's bed wasn't slept in last night. Gyp Clyde was at the desk all night an' he said Wade didn't come in after supper. That forged note was the bait for a man trap, Curly."

Curly Joyce had saddled her claybank pony while the lawman had been investigating Wade's hotel room. She mounted and was waiting in the street by the time Rocky Donovan emerged from the stable lean-to behind the jail house, where he kept his dun mustang.

"What on earth can we do first?" moaned the girl, desperation making her voice crack. "We know Hal was lured out of town late last night by this fake note. But where? Where?"

Rocky Donovan's jaw thrust out grimly.

"Redfern knows the answers, of course," snarled the lawman, with a baleful glare at Redfern's Blue Skull Saloon. "But he'd just laugh at me if I asked him any questions. He'd have an alibi for where he was last night."

Donovan glanced at Paydirt Patterson, who was mounted on his own saddle horse alongside Curly Joyce. Despair was mirrored in the glances the two men exchanged.

"Only clue I see to work on," said Donovan, "is Sam Smith. He's been a lone-wolf prospector all his life, but last I knew he was workin' for Bret Redfern out at the Lucky Lode. We'll ride out there an' see if we can make him talk."

They galloped out of town, heading due north along a well-worn trail which led off through the Badluck ridges toward the vast gold and silver claims owned by Bret Redfern.

It was ten o'clock before they reached the cluster of tarpaper-covered shacks where Redfern's big mining crew lived. Most of the workmen were underground, gouging out treasure ore.

A stamp mill was working, crushing rock. There, Rocky Donovan sought out a red-whiskered hardrocker who was Redfern's mine foreman, Dummy Edmonds.

When he returned to where Patterson and Curly Joyce waited on the trail, Donovan's face was grim.

"Edmonds told me that Sam Smith left the Lucky Lode diggin's two days ago, and ain't been back since," rasped the marshal. "I'm dead sure Smith wasn't in Deadhorse last night, because I made the rounds of every joint in town several times myself."

A feeling of hopelessness overcame the three of them, as they headed silently back through the hills toward Deadhorse.

Donovan had every reason to believe Edmonds' story that Sam Smith was not on duty at Redfern's stamp mill. The lawman had known Edmonds for years, knew that his word was good, even if he did work for a criminal of Redfern's ilk.

"It's worse than huntin' for a needle in the proverbial haystack," groaned Rocky Donovan, when they had left the hubbub of the Lucky Lode mine behind them. "Because in this case, we ain't even got a haystack to hunt in."

Curly Joyce rubbed her throat with both hands, struggling to stem the torrent of emotion which had gripped her. Donovan and Patterson, sensing her agitation and guessing why, kept their eyes on the trail.

But Curly Joyce, although she ramrodded a stagecoach line and performed a man's task here on the Western frontier, was, after all, a woman.

A moment later, the three came to a halt on the trail and stood in the sweltering sunshine while Curly Joyce leaned from saddle to sob out her heart on Rocky Donovan's shoulder.

"You're in love with Hal Wade, ain't you,

girl?" whispered the old tinstar, blinking his own eyes.

"More than . . . than . . . life itself," she whispered huskily, pulling herself together with an effort. "But—we're not getting anywhere standing here, Rocky. What will we do? What can we do? It's tearing the heart out of me, knowing that this very minute Hal may be lying murdered somewhere. He . . . he—"

The girl's face went suddenly hard, and she dropped a hand to the ivory stock of a Colt .45.

"Rocky," she said in a dispassionate monotone, "I'm going to kill Bret Redfern. He's back of this. I'll never see Hal Wade alive again—I know that. But I'm going to kill the man who murdered him. I . . . I don't want you to think I'm loco, Rocky. And after . . . after I'm through with Redfern . . . I don't care what you do to me."

Donovan tried to speak, but could find no answer to the girl's outburst. He spurred on ahead, Curly Joyce following between his horse and Patterson's.

The sun climbed to the noon position in the sky, as they headed back toward the main trail leading to Deadhorse town.

And it was Rocky Donovan whose steely eyes, raking the surrounding malpais, caught sight of the three tiny black dots which wheeled to the southward, a mile high in the brassy sky.

He halted his horse instinctively, a hand uplifted to shade his eyes against the glare of the sun.

Paydirt Patterson and Curly Joyce spotted the wheeling buzzards, then. Three almost invisible dots in the sky, describing ever-lowering circles as they soared in the cloudless dome of the heavens around a common center.

"*Zopilote* hawks," husked out the marshal. "They've spotted a dead calf in Cal Bozeman's pasture, I reckon."

Curly Joyce jerked up her reins.

"Those buzzards are too far east to be flying over Bozeman's range," she said in a voice that was no longer unsteady. "Come on, boys. We've got to get over there—before those buzzards—get to earth—"

A common thought gripped the three friends as they spurred their jaded mounts into a hard gallop, working their way southward toward the focal point of those circling birds of prey.

Natural scavengers were buzzards. Their telescopic vision enabled them to spot even a dead fieldmouse from tremendous heights.

But no fieldmouse or maverick's carcass would be at the bottom of those spirals. The wings of death were hovering over a human corpse. Donovan knew it. Curly knew it. Patterson knew it.

And they knew, as they fought their way through a sunbaked wilderness of lava fields and upflung cliffs and barren, brushless desolation, that the buzzards had spotted a dead man far outside the zone of mining operations.

Two hours later, they topped the last rise to find themselves overlooking the bleak ravine known to the miners as Dead Man's Gulch.

Like a guiding beacon, the ever-lowering buzzards had led them to the spot. The red-necked, heavy-beaked carrion birds were tugging at something down in the bottom of the ravine as the riders skidded their horses down a fresh scar on the hillside where an avalanche had exposed naked bedrock.

When the earth and rock became too soft for the horses to travel over, the two men and the girl dismounted and slogged their way toward the spot where the four buzzards were flapping and tearing away at their feast.

"You . . . you wait here, Curly!" ordered Rocky Donovan. "Mind what I say, girl!"

Curly Joyce slumped to her knees, obeying the marshal's harsh-voiced but kindly order.

Paydirt Patterson and the lawman waded through the fresh avalanche pile and looked down on the human carrion that had attracted the birds which now angrily wheeled and dipped in the sweltering air above the gulch.

They were looking at the mutilated legs of a dead man, half covered by rock and earth.

A gusty sigh of relief coursed through Rocky

Donovan as he dug away earth and rubble to expose the corpse's buried head, then yelled over to Curly Joyce:

"Buck up, girl. It ain't Hal Wade. This dead man is Sam Smith, and he didn't get killed in no rockslide by accident. There's a bullet hole in his forehead."

—Chapter XXII—

Corpse for a Tombstone

Leaving Sam Smith's half-buried corpse, the two men walked back to where Curly sat on the avalanche heap, legs curled beneath her. They squatted down, placing themselves in such a way that her eyes would be spared the gruesome spectacle of the dead mucker.

"Buck up, Curly," repeated the lawman. "We've got some tall thinking to do."

With an effort, the girl lifted tear-misted eyes to meet the marshal's sympathetic gaze.

"This . . . this doesn't bring us any closer to solving the mystery of Hal's disappearance," she whispered.

The old lawman scratched the fresh earth underfoot with a horny forefinger, studying the landscape with expert eyes.

"I ain't so sure," Donovan commented. "We know that Sam Smith guided Hal Wade out of town last night—guided him to a trap. We're pretty sure of that; right?"

The girl nodded.

"O.K. We've found Smith. He was murdered. Or shot, anyway. Now, did Hal Wade kill Smith? I got my doubts."

The grizzled old marshal got to his feet, leaving Paydirt Patterson to comfort the girl. For the better part of twenty minutes the lawman prowled about, studying the terrain.

When he returned from a second inspection of Smith's corpse, he extended his hand. In the leathery cup of his palm were several shreds of pink-colored paper, some of them burned slightly at the edges, but all of them shredded.

"Look here," he said. "This paper—you recognize it, Paydirt? As a minin' man, you ought to."

Patterson inspected the tissue-thin paper fragments, and nodded.

"Sure. This was wrappin' off a dynamite stick."

Donovan nodded. Then he pointed up the hillside to where the avalanche had cleaned off a section of Dead Man's Gully, exposing native bedrock.

"See this avalanche? It's about ten yards wide, and it piled up this dirt where we're sittin'. It almost buried Sam Smith—from the looks of things, Smith's corpse was carried a ways by the rockslide itself. And scattered here and there over this fresh earth I found these wrappin's of a stick of dynamite."

Curly Joyce nodded understanding of Donovan's findings, but the haunted look did not die out of her eyes.

"You know what happened?" went on Donovan. "This avalanche was no accident. A dynamite blast set it off. The wrappin' paper of the dynamite stick blew up in the air an', bein' light, floated down slower than the rock and earth come down."

The marshal jerked a thumb toward Smith's corpse.

"Where Smith fits into the picture, I don't know—except I got a hunch some other party shot him after he'd set off the dynamite fuse, just to keep him from tellin' *why* that avalanche was started."

Paydirt Patterson jumped to his feet with an oath.

"There could only be one reason for setting a rock slide to rollin'," he cried. "That would be—to cover up something—"

A low cry escaped Curly Joyce's lips.

"To cover . . . up . . . evidence of murder!" she whispered. "Rocky—something tells me—Hal's under this pile of dirt."

Patterson met Donovan's gaze, above and behind the girl's head. They both nodded, as the grim significance of their discovery took meaning.

"We'll soon make sure," panted the Red Eagle mine owner. "Curly, we're only a couple of miles from my mine. I've got forty-odd men workin' over there. I'll bring 'em here—we'll bring mules and wheelbarrows—we'll uncover this pile of dirt before sundown—and make certain if we've found Hal Wade's grave—"

• • •

The rest of the afternoon was a nightmare to Curly Joyce. She stationed herself on the south ridge of the gulch, where an outcrop of limestone and slate formation shielded her from the pitiless rays of the westering sun.

Down in the bottom of the gully, smoke boiled up from a scene as stirring and bustling as a gold rush could ever be.

Red-shirted miners, Irishmen and Vermont Yankees and Chinamen and swart-skinned Mexicans, toiled with shovels and wheelbarrows as they cleared away the mound of debris caused by the mysterious landslide.

Miners and drillers from Paydirt Patterson's

Red Eagle outfit, they worked with a lusty will, as if golden reward lay beneath that rock heap. But it was not gold they dug for, but a dead man—a dead man who was already assuming the proportions
of a popular hero in Deadhorse—Hal Wade, the Rocking R trail boss from the border country.

As afternoon shadows began to pool in the brushy depths of Dead Man's Gulch, long lines of mules were plodding away to east and west, depositing tons of earth along the pit of the gulch.

They reached the broken brambles of chaparral which told them they had uncovered the former bottom of the dry wash. Each passing moment, Curly Joyce steeled herself for the fateful instant when Paydirt Patterson or the kindly old marshal would order the miners to quit working.

Then she would be led gently down the slope to look on the broken, mangled body of the man she loved.

But they found no dead man. Shovels cleared away earth and boulders, to expose the weather-beaten timbers of an old mine tunnel.

Grimly, Patterson ordered his sweating, exhausted men to clean out the dirt that had spilled into the tunnel. They kept apprehensive eyes on Curly Joyce, who sat with averted gaze on the crest of the southern ridge.

Came the moment, at sundown time, when a strange hush filled the air. The clang of shovels on rock ceased, as if at a signal. Mules halted their plodding journeys to and from the various mounds of cleared-away débris.

Digging fingernails into her palms, Curly Joyce forced herself to look down into the shadow-filled gully. She saw Paydirt Patterson emerging from the mine tunnel, saw him look up at her, arm lifted in a wave.

"I know . . . I know—" she told herself, shutting her eyes against the tableau below. "They've found Hal—they don't want me to look at his body—"

But there was a glad note in the Red Eagle mine owner's voice, as he shouted up the slope at her:

"Get down here fast, girl! Get down here—we've found him—Hal Wade."

From the depths of the mine tunnel came Rocky Donovan's ghostly yell:

"You damned fool, Patterson—tell Curly he's alive! *Alive!* Tell her that, before she goes crazy!"

Running headlong down the slope, falling and picking herself up again, oblivious to scratches and bruises, Curly Joyce reached the pit of Dead Man's Gulch as Rocky Donovan and one of the Red Eagle miners emerged from the narrow tunnel, bearing a limp body between them.

Unable to speak, unable to find relief in tears, Curly Joyce flung herself on her knees beside Hal Wade, caught his limp head to her breast, crushed her lips hysterically to his.

"Fresh air'll revive him pronto, girl," Rocky Donovan choked. "But five minutes later would have been too late—"

—Chapter XXIII—

DEAD MAN'S SOMBRERO

Shortly before midnight that night Scorchy Langlie tooled his Thunderbolt Express coach into Bret Redfern's livery barn and turned the jaded team over to a half-breed *mozo* for handling.

His duties done for the day, the hard-bitten old jehu headed down the night-shrouded street toward the Blue Skull Saloon to make his usual report to Redfern.

Three men emerged from the Bonanza Hotel across the street and started westward in the direction Langlie was taking. The old stage driver took one look at the three hombres, noting their purposeful strides, recognizing their voices.

Then, with a startled oath, Scorchy Langlie ducked into an alley and sprinted with all the speed his aged and rheumatic limbs could muster up, to the back of the Blue Skull Saloon.

Light glowed from the window of Bret Redfern's private office. Langlie hurried across the back porch, entered a black hallway, and a moment later was hammering excitedly on the door of Redfern's office. A voice challenged him from within; then, when Langlie had identified himself, the door was unlocked and opened by Black Bill Collier.

Seated at his desk in mid-room was Redfern himself.

"What's got you all lathered up, Scorchy?" asked Redfern, frowning at the interruption.

The oldster jabbed a brittle finger toward the main street.

"You're goin' to have visitors, boss, unless I miss my guess. Rocky Donovan an' the coroner, Doc Phelps, an'—"

Redfern waved him off, the cheroot in his fingers leaving a figure 8 trail of smoke in the stuffy air.

"Let 'em come!" he jeered. "The law never has anything to hang on me, Scorchy. You ought to know that by now."

But the old driver's next words burst like a bombshell:

"Yeah? Well, guess who's *with* that tinstar an' doc! The feller you told me was dead—buried alive yesterday in Sam Smith's old mine—*Hal Wade!*"

Redfern sat up with a thump, his teeth wedging through the thick cigar and almost biting it in two.

"Hal Wade? Alive?"

Langlie nodded, and continued breathlessly: "Not only that, but Doc Phelps is carryin' a blue beaver Stetson in his hand—a hat with a bundle o' snake rattles on the band. That'll be Sam Smith's skypiece, won't it?"

Black Bill Collier staggered past Langlie and placed his palsied hands on Redfern's desk. His voice trembled with fear:

"Chief, we got to vamoose out of here. Something went wrong, if what Langlie says is the truth. We've got to—"

Redfern was about to silence Collier with an impatient oath when a loud knock sounded on the door leading to the front barroom.

"Vamoose, Scorchy!" whispered Redfern sharply. "Thanks for tippin' me off what to expect. You, Collier—open the door. We won't run—for hell or high water or Hal Wade's ghost. Hurry!"

The knock was repeated, followed by Marshal Donovan's voice as the lawman rattled the doorknob.

Old Langlie hastened out of the office by the rear door.

Black Bill Collier, his face pasty with fear, fingered the twin derringers which he kept in clip holsters under either cuff.

"Open up, Redfern!" thundered Donovan. "I got business."

Redfern threw back his coattails to bare his guns. Collier went to the door and threw it wide.

Framed in the doorway was Rocky Donovan, his mouth clamped into a line as thin and immovable as a crack in a boulder. At his right elbow was white-haired old Doc Phelps, holding a blue beaver Stetson in his hand. Hal Wade was nowhere to be seen.

They stepped inside and shut the door. Then, before Bret Redfern knew what was coming, the lawman's right hand flashed to his hip and came up with a six-gun.

Instead of pointing it in Redfern's general direction, as his eyes would have indicated, Rocky Donovan swung the cocked .45 to the right and jammed the barrel into Black Bill Collier's side.

Redfern's hands started to slide back off his desk, but a second gun appeared magically in Donovan's left and its bore leveled at the saloon keeper's chest.

"No booger moves, now, either of you!" snapped the marshal. "Doc, ask Redfern if he recognizes that hat."

The coroner strode forward and tossed the battered and dusty Stetson on Redfern's desk. The hat was sticky with clotted blood, and there was a bullet hole piercing the band where it nestled against the rear of the brim.

"What's the idea?" snarled Redfern, his face chalky-white. "Whose hat's that?"

For answer, Doc Phelps reached in a vest pocket and fished out a pellet of lead incased in a jacket of copper-alloy steel.

"The hat belonged to a man working at the

Lucky Lode stamp mill—Sam Smith," clipped Doc Phelps. "That blob of lead there happens to be a slug from a .25/3000 Winchester rifle. I dug it out of Smith's corpse less than twenty minutes ago."

Bret Redfern started to reach for the misshapen bullet, but the coroner snatched it back and pocketed it.

Black Bill Collier was trembling visibly, his eyes glued to the gun barrel which the marshal still held against his body. But Donovan's flinty gaze was riveted on Redfern, noticing every twitch of the saloon man's facial muscles, analyzing every changing emotion registered on the killer's countenance.

"You've been a slick one, Redfern!" tolled Donovan's voice. "You got title to the Lucky Lode Mine by murderin' the prospectors who rightfully owned it. You—"

"That's a lie!" Redfern's voice cracked, like that of a man backed to the wall and knowing that doom lies ahead.

"Maybe so—I don't claim to be able to prove it. You've been waxing rich off of this Blue Skull Saloon, robbing miners of their gold dust with your crooked faro and red dog and poker and roulette—"

"You can't prove—"

"Hell, I don't have to prove it!" roared the marshal. "I'm just telling you that you've been plenty slick, blocking the law at every turn. I won't even mention the slick way you burned the Wells Fargo office and tried to murder Rex Joyce—the way you bushwhacked Jimmy O'Niel in the *Observer* office—the way you wrecked Curly's stagecoach, the fake Indian raid you made on the Boothill Express, the way you switched corpses—"

Redfern stood up, his face terrible to see. Well he knew that Rocky Donovan was not standing here talking to him for the fun of seeing him squirm. Donovan was a man of action, not talk.

"All right—what's all this got to do with you bargin' in here with Sam Smith's hat and throwin' a bullet on my desk?" shouted Redfern, his voice thick with anger. "You can't pin any killing on me. Why should I kill one of my own miners? Especially an insignificant booze swilling mucker like Sam Smith?"

Rocky Donovan's grin was not pleasant to see. He had waited a long time for this moment, and he was enjoying it to the dregs.

"Redfern, you own the only .25/3000-calibered gun in the whole Washoe country. Long range, but light—that's what you need in your dry-gulch game. Your rifle killed Sam Smith—"

Redfern seemed to relax. When the going got rough, the outlaw's nerves were coolest. But the thing that was hammering his brain was—where did Hal Wade fit into the picture? Langlie had said Wade accompanied the marshal tonight. Had Langlie been seeing things?

"The caliber of my guns won't be evidence in court, Donovan," sneered Redfern. "You got to have witnesses to back your talk."

Rocky Donovan laughed harshly.

"Doc, put the handcuffs on Redfern. We got a good witness, Redfern. That witness happens to be Hal Wade!"

If Donovan had expected his revelation of Wade's still being alive to surprise Redfern, he was disappointed.

Doc Phelps took a pair of wrist irons from his pocket and started around the desk toward Redfern.

The latter lifted his hands as if to receive the manacles. Then, in a movement incredibly fast, Bret Redfern seized the aged medico by one arm. As he hauled Phelps in front of him, Redfern's other hand got a .45 six-gun from the holster.

Rocky Donovan leaped to place his own body behind Collier, even as Redfern thumbed back his gun hammer. Collier screamed:

"Don't shoot, chief! You'd kill me instead!"

Doc Phelps grunted with horror as he felt Redfern drag him backward toward the rear door. Rocky Donovan cursed angrily, as he realized that to shoot at Redfern would mean sure death for his friend, the coroner.

Kicking open the door behind him, Redfern

shoved Phelps violently forward. Before the old medico had dropped out of the line of fire, the door slammed and the back corridor rang to the sound of Redfern's retreating footsteps.

Redfern wondered why Donovan or Phelps made no effort at pursuit, as he sped out across the back porch at top speed.

Then, too late to check his headlong rush, Redfern saw that the marshal had an ace in the hole.

Blocking his path of escape stood Hal Wade, a spread-legged phantom in the gloom of the backyard.

Wade's right fist traveled up in a perfectly-timed haymaker even as Bret Redfern whipped up his six-gun.

The cowboy's fist smashed into Redfern's ribs above the heart, the combined force of the blow and Redfern's onrushing speed paralyzing the outlaw before he could trigger his Colt .45.

Knocked cold, Redfern sprawled headlong in a battered heap at Wade's feet.

The man from Arizona gave a short, brittle laugh as he stared down at the inert huddle. Then he lifted his voice to yell inside the saloon:

"Everything's *bueno*, boys. Redfern's waitin' for the irons."

Unseen in the shadows, Scorchy Langlie fingered a six-gun, but dared not shoot because Wade was invisible in the darkness. Langlie decided it would be best to hold his fire, bide his time.

A moment later, Doc Phelps groped his way outdoors. Handcuffs clicked—and Bret Redfern was under arrest for the first time in his notorious career.

—Chapter XXIV—

Marked for Boothill

"What did you hit him with, man?" panted the coroner, as he and Wade carried the unconscious Redfern back into the saloon hallway and headed for the office where Donovan waited. "When a man's wilted like this, he's either dead or got brain concussion!"

Hal Wade chuckled as he opened the office door with a boot.

"I reckon the shock of seeing me alive helped put him out," commented the Arizonan.

They deposited Redfern's slumped form on the floor. Still crouched across the room was the marshal of Deadhorse, his six-gun jammed in Black Bill Collier's midriff.

"You ain't got anything on me, Donovan!" stammered the lantern-jawed gambler, his eyes glazed with panic. "I didn't have nothin' to do with Redfern clappin' Wade in that tunnel!"

Donovan frisked the gambler deftly, producing a belted Colt in addition to the pair of single-barreled derringers hidden under Collier's shirt cuffs.

"You'll stretch hang rope for not reporting

Wade's predicament to me, then," rasped Donovan, taking out a pair of handcuffs. "You can count yourself lucky I didn't plug you when Redfern tried to vamoose. But I knew Wade would take care of your boss out back."

Collier groaned. It seemed impossible that he and Redfern could be captured without a shot being fired, with none of their bodyguards in the front barroom knowing of the drama enacted in Redfern's back office.

But it had happened. Showdown had come. And twenty minutes later, unknown to the town's residents, the unconscious Bret Redfern and his henchman, Collier, were safely locked in the rock-walled Deadhorse jail house.

Redfern was still out cold. It was Phelps' professional belief that the boss outlaw would remain unconscious for several hours to come, as a result of the terrific blow to the heart which Hal Wade had administered to block Redfern's attempt at a getaway.

"Well, gents, that's that!" chuckled the marshal, as the three men paused in the marshal's front office to say good night. "It's been a busy day, an' Wade went through a hell of an ordeal. But seein' as how we've finally got enough on Redfern an' Collier to hang 'em, I reckon you figger it was worth bein' buried alive for, eh, Wade?"

The cowboy from Arizona grinned heartily.

"I'm not kickin'," he said. "I reckon the happiest moment of my mangy life was when I woke up and saw open sky overhead instead of darkness—"

Doc Phelps chuckled audibly:

"—and lookin' up into Curly Joyce's face wasn't exactly a nightmare," the medico cut in. "That kiss she give you, just as you were comin' to, would have put life into a brass man!"

Hitching his chaps belt, Wade made his way across the darkened street to the Bonanza Hotel. He had enjoyed a big meal at Paydirt Patterson's gold-mine cook house, on the way back to Deadhorse that night; but the prospect of hitting the hay seemed plenty welcome indeed.

Curly Joyce and her father were waiting for him in the hotel lobby, before going upstairs to their own living quarters. Their attitude of tense waiting relaxed at his entrance, for both had protested against Wade's desire to witness Donovan's arrest of the Blue Skull Saloon outlaws.

"Well, it's all over, amigos!" Wade informed them. "Rocky's got both of those polecats in jail, and he says it won't take more'n a week to get a kangaroo-court trial over with and make 'em do a jig at the end of a rope."

Rex Joyce wagged his bandaged head doubtfully.

"I won't sleep good until Collier an' Redfern are planted in a boothill box," the Wells Fargo man grunted. "An' don't sleep too close to an open window these nights, Hal. You're the key witness against those hombres, and they got plenty of ambushers on their payroll who'll get a fat bonus if they put you out of the way before the trial."

Wade accompanied them upstairs, and walked down the hall toward his own room.

He was well aware of the fact that he would be a marked man for dry-gulch lead, once Redfern's henchmen learned of their chief's arrest and imprisonment on murder charges.

It would pay him to take Rex Joyce's advice and move his bed well away from the open window overlooking the side street, Wade realized as he opened his bedroom door.

Even as he stepped into the semidarkness of his room, a sixth sense seemed to warn him of peril lurking in the shadows. He cast off the apprehensive feeling, knowing that danger could not exist this soon after Redfern's arrest. After all, only ten minutes had elapsed since Redfern had been knocked out in his desperate bid for escape, over at the saloon. Nobody knew—

And then the swift scrape of a shoe sole over the floor boards behind him made Hal Wade spin about.

Dim light flashed on a knife blade wielded by a charging figure who had crouched against the dark curtains of a corner closet.

Razor-edged steel sliced like molten fire along Wade's ribs as the bowie's point probed at his heart.

Only the fact that a throw rug slipped under his attacker's charging feet saved Wade's life.

Wade lashed out a jabbing left fist. The two went down in a heap, rolling over and over in a grapple until they struck a bedpost. Then they reared to their feet, Wade trying desperately to seize the killer's wrist and turn aside the vicious chopping motions of the knife.

Blood gushed from the long gash along his chest, smearing the killer's cheek as they wrestled silently in the darkness.

Whiskey-fouled breath nauseated Wade as he tripped his adversary and they crashed to the floor once more.

Putting every ounce of his flagging strength into breaking the bushwhacker's grip on his knife, Wade felt the man's other hand clamp thumb and fingers on his windpipe.

The knife fell from the killer's paralyzed wrist, was kicked aside under scuffling feet as the cowboy felt the air shut off from his lungs.

A knee smashed against his groin, sickening him with pain. Desperately, Wade broke free of the strangling grip and lashed out a smoking haymaker that would have knocked out his foe if it had landed.

But the knifeman, realizing that his desperate attempt at stabbing Wade had failed, now lurched back, clawing at a six-gun in his belt.

Himself unarmed, Hal Wade twisted sideways and jerked up a chair, hurtling it with all his force at the shadowy figure even as light from the open window glinted off naked gun steel.

The chair smashed into kindling wood, knocking the gun out of the killer's grasp and making him grunt with agony.

Then, turning, the would-be assassin fled for the window, Wade at his heels.

Too late, the cowboy snatched at the prowler's arm. The man wrenched free, leaving part of his sleeve in Wade's fingers. He landed on the short side porch outside, raced to the edge of the roof, and dropped from sight in the black alley below.

Wade sprang after him, then paused with his legs forking the window sill.

The outlaw might be squatting in the darkness below with another gun, ready to skyline him against the porch roof. To show himself now would be to invite sure death.

Panting heavily with exertion, his throat aching where fingers had gouged deep bruises in the flesh of his neck, Hal Wade ducked back inside and jerked down the window shade.

He lighted a lamp, and inspected his disheveled

face in the blistered mirror of a bureau across the room.

"Redfern's men work fast," he panted to himself. "One thing certain, they got me marked for boothill."

He stared at the bit of red cloth in his fingers, cloth he had ripped from the assassin's sleeve. He tried to remember where he had seen that color shirt before. But it was a common hue among the Nevada miners.

Then he picked up the blood-stained bowie knife he had wrested from the outlaw's grasp at the outset of the melee. Etched with gun-bluing acid on the gore-smeared steel were the fancy, intertwined initials "S. L."

"Scorchy Langlie!" panted Wade in a hoarse whisper. "He's the stage jehu that came battin' out of Redfern's office a couple of ticks before Donovan smoked Redfern out of his den. He must have rattled his hocks right over to my hotel room here to wait for me—"

The knowledge that he was bucking desperate odds chilled Wade. As old Rex Joyce had warned him, he was the key witness on whose testimony a court would sentence Redfern and Collier to die.

The outlaw element of Deadhorse, rallying behind their jailed leader, would spare no effort to kill Wade in the days to follow. Not one moment, asleep or awake, would he be safe from attack.

Langlie's ill-fated attempt to murder him tonight would be but a prelude to peril. But the stake was worth the risk. Once Redfern was out of the way, Deadhorse town would be free of its yoke of lawlessness. And Curly Joyce would be free of the Boothill Express reputation which dogged her stagecoach business—

Curly Joyce! Remembering the girl's kiss as he was struggling his way out of a smothered coma, that evening as he was lifted out of Sam Smith's deserted mine, Hal Wade realized that Curly Joyce had unknowingly slapped her brand on his hide for keeps.

—Chapter XXV—

Frontier Kangaroo Court

Mining operations came to a standstill in the hectic week that followed.

News of Bret Redfern's arrest on charges of murder quickly spread to the outermost reaches of the Badluck country which made Deadhorse its focal center of trading and carousing.

As a result of the event which even old-timers agreed was the most sensational happening ever to transpire in the Washoe country since the discovery of the Comstock Lode—the forthcoming kangaroo-court trial—the gold camp was jammed with humanity.

Entire crews were laid off on the bigger outfits—the Wilderness, the Lucky Lode, the Red Eagle—and flocked into town the day following Redfern's arrest.

The Blue Skull Saloon significantly enough, padlocked its doors. The Thunderbolt Express stabled its coaches, corralled its teams. Redfern's enterprises had reached a standstill, pending the fate of their owner.

Business for Wells Fargo boomed as a result.

Whip Gleason took out freight and mail every other day, and his Concord was loaded with excited passengers on every return trip.

Hal Wade, on whose person was focused the main interest of the crowds, was kept under constant guard by men deputized for bodyguard duty by Rocky Donovan. The marshal was taking no chance on a second attempt being made to murder his main witness.

It would not be an official trial, since legal jurisprudence was not operating in Nevada. It would be a frontier kangaroo court, presided over by grizzled old Alamo Burkett, who had been a New England judge before coming West for the gold rush.

Because Deadhorse had no courthouse, Burkett decided to stage the kangaroo court in a deserted saloon known as the Silver Dollar.

The saloon's bar became the bench of justice; its barroom was crowded with benches, boxes, beer barrels and other impromptu seating arrangements for those lucky enough to witness the proceedings.

On the fourth morning after Redfern's arrest, Judge Alamo Burkett hammered the bar of the Silver Dollar Saloon with the butt of a six-gun in lieu of a gavel, and in a clear, compelling, powerful voice called court in session.

Rocky Donovan and his deputies had been careful to divest all spectators of six-guns, knives, or other weapons. In so far as was possible, he forbade entrance to any men known to be paid gun hawks in Redfern's employ; the marshal had no intention of having his prisoners rescued by a slaughtering crew of outlaws.

A jury was chosen of twelve miners and prospectors, none of them working for the defendant's Lucky Lode outfit, men who would listen to the testimony offered with an impartial ear.

Curly Joyce and her father, Whip Gleason, Paydirt Patterson, and Ralph Neeley obtained seats in the coveted front row. Between them and the bar counter had been placed two baize-covered poker tables, one for the prosecution, the other for the defense.

Outside the jammed courtroom, hundreds of miners, Indians, gamblers, riffraff and visitors from Carson City rubbed elbows in a jam which filled the main street from wall to wall. Donovan had sworn in an even twenty deputies, armed them with sawed-off shotguns, and mounted them on horses. They had orders to maintain order outdoors.

Redfern and Collier, handcuffed and under a heavy guard of mounted deputies recruited from Patterson's gold mine, were escorted from the nearby jail building to the courtroom. A buzz of excitement grew to bedlam as the two notorious prisoners came in through a door adjoining the back-bar mirror and were escorted to the defendants' table.

Their defense lawyer was none other than peppery-voiced Scorchy Langlie, who before becoming a stage driver for Redfern's Thunderbolt Express Co. had been an attorney-at-law. There were some who hinted that Langlie had skipped out of California a couple of jumps ahead of a vigilante committee, before he had come to Nevada and traded a briefcase for a horsewhip.

By the morning of the fifth day following Redfern's imprisonment, however, the trial which was to become one of the most spectacular in the West's lurid history was under way.

Hal Wade, as chief witness for the prosecution, was called to the stand first. He gave a graphic account of Sam Smith's luring him to a mantrap by means of a letter bearing Paydirt Patterson's forged signature.

Curly Joyce had turned over the letter in question to Rocky Donovan, who submitted it to the court and backed it with Patterson's sworn testimony that he had not written it.

Wade then described being slugged by Sam Smith and taken to a ravine known as Dead Man's Gulch, where he was met by Bret Redfern and Black Bill Collier.

Despite Scorchy Langlie's leering taunts to the effect that the court could not accept Wade's word against that of Collier and Redfern—who claimed to have an iron-tight alibi that they had been playing roulette in the Blue Skull Saloon at the time—Judge Burkett allowed the testimony to be heard.

Then Curly Joyce, the marshal, and Paydirt Patterson were each called to the witness stand in turn, to describe how they had discovered Sam Smith's corpse in the avalanche heap; the evidence that the rockslide had been caused by a dynamite blast; and the subsequent discovery of Hal Wade, entombed alive in the abandoned mine tunnel.

Dr. Zebediah Phelps, an official coroner, produced the fatal bullet which had killed Sam Smith and voiced his certainty that it had been fired by Bret Redfern's .25/3000 Winchester.

Phelps also described Redfern's attempted escape the night after Wade's rescue when Donovan had confronted the outlaw in his saloon office.

Rocky Donovan, summing up the case against Redfern and Collier, hinted at Redfern's long domination of Deadhorse and his many attacks on the Wells Fargo Co.'s so-called Boothill Express. These remarks, however, were overruled and stricken off the record by the judge, as having no bearing on the present case against the defendants.

Scorchy Langlie, with very eloquent oratory, pointed out in rebuttal that there was no shred of evidence against either Redfern or Collier; that their alibi was unshaken; and that the judge and jury only had Hal Wade's word to prove that the defendants were guilty.

Thus it was, shortly before sundown, that Judge Alamo Burkett sent the jury into a back room of the Silver Dollar Saloon that had once served as a poker den, to deliberate and return with a verdict.

The judge's legal mind told him that Donovan and Wade actually had not proved that the defendants had buried Wade alive in a mine tunnel, nor was there actual proof that Redfern had fired the shot that had killed Sam Smith.

But this was no ordinary trial. This was in Nevada's wildest gold camp; and it was common knowledge to everyone, including Judge Burkett, that Bret Redfern was an owlhooter of the first water, facing trial for the first time in his notorious career.

After being closeted for less than five minutes, the jury filed grimly out into the barroom, to face the hushed mob in the makeshift court-house.

Redfern, his beady eyes fixed on the foreman of the jury, read his doom in the latter's face. Black Bill Collier sat moodily beside his chief, staring down at the handcuffs which manacled his wrists.

"The jury's verdict," called out the foreman without waiting for the judge to ask him to report, "is that the defendants are guiltier'n hell and should be hung by the neck—"

The roar of excitement in the courtroom was carried quickly to the waiting mob which packed the street outside, and Rocky Donovan's deputies had a nervous moment as the air was rocked with gunfire—the method many a case-hardened miner had of letting off steam.

When order was finally restored, Judge Burkett stood up behind the brass-railed bar of justice and tapped the counter with his six-gun butt.

"The prisoners will stand before the bar to receive sentence," he intoned in a sepulchral voice.

Hal Wade glanced around at Curly Joyce, saw the girl holding the sides of her chair in an ecstasy of suspense. Their big moment had arrived; the destiny of Wells Fargo hung in the balance.

Bret Redfern and Black Bill Collier got to their feet, their heads erect and eyes flashing with defiance as they walked around their table and stood in front of the judge behind the liquor bar.

"A jury having found you guilty as charged of the attempted murder of Hal Wade and the murder of one Sam Smith," said the judge in a voice which crackled in the far corners of the death-hushed room, "I hereby sentence you to be hanged by the neck until dead, at a place which Marshal Donovan shall designate, time for said execution to be not later than—"

And then, with the eyes of every person in the room riveted to the judge's lips, something happened which could have happened, it seemed, only in a fantastic dream.

Scorchy Langlie leaped to his feet and stamped his right boot sharply on the floor of the saloon.

Instantly, a rectangular hole yawned in the floor where Redfern and Collier were standing before the bar of justice—the trapdoor to a whiskey cellar beneath the floor of the saloon which served as a courtroom!

Hal Wade, staring incredulously, saw the two outlaws vanish from sight in the black depths of the cellar.

He leaped forward, Rocky Donovan at his side.

Before the stunned courtroom mob knew what was happening, Scorchy Langlie leaped forward, his shoulders crashing against the lawman and Hal Wade and propelling them bodily into the black hole in the floor.

An instant later Langlie himself had leaped out of sight beneath the level of the floor.

Shots rang out underground, followed by a yell of horror and agony from the unseen marshal. Then invisible hands closed the trapdoor, and the heavy planks concealed the destiny of the vanished prisoners and Rocky Donovan and Hal Wade.

—Chapter XXVI—

Oath to a Tinstar

In the mad, peril-packed instant of time that Hal Wade felt himself hurled bodily into the yawning trapdoor in the floor of the improvised courtroom, he had no chance to adjust himself against catastrophe.

He had a brief, blurred glimpse of a pile of cushioning gunnysacks rushing up to slam him in the face as he and Rocky Donovan were plunged headlong from the floor above by Scorchy Langlie's propelling arms.

Instinct told the cowboy to roll sideways into black gloom the instant he landed on the burlap heap which, barely two seconds before, had absorbed the shock of falling for Bret Redfern and Black Bill Collier.

He saw Rocky Donovan try to pick himself up, even as Wade himself rolled out of the bar of light cast by the lamps in the saloon overhead.

In that brief clock-tick of time he glimpsed Scorchy Langlie jumping down into the cellar to land partly on top of Donovan's body, knocking the dazed marshal flat against the heaped-up gunnysacks.

Then from behind the hinged trapdoor which

hung from the floor beam overhead, men unseen in the darkness shoved against the door and slammed it shut.

"Get Wade!"

It was Redfern's voice, hissing from the darkness somewhere beyond.

A shot blasted deafeningly from the point where two men had slammed shut the trapdoor.

A bullet kicked dirt in Wade's face as he continued rolling violently along the earthen floor of the liquor cellar. Two more shots rang out as gun flashes stabbed the darkness. Killers were triggering lead into the spot where Wade's body had lain an instant before the trapdoor slammed to seal the cellar in gloom.

On the heels of the ear-stunning gunfire came a scream of agony from Rocky Donovan.

Then, for a brief second, ghastly stillness. It was interrupted by a rumble of booted feet in the courtroom overhead, as the stunned crowd finally snapped out of their trance and went into action.

Hal Wade's brain was working like a lightning bolt. As yet, no slug had touched him. But he must keep moving!

He brought up sharply against a cobwebby case of beer bottles, and the empty bottles jangled musically. Sharp intakes of breath came from elsewhere in the room, followed by a long, quivering moan which Hal Wade knew came from Rocky Donovan.

“Get going!” came Redfern’s voice, low pitched and as venomous as a sidewinder’s hiss. “That pack of skunks will be down here in another couple of ticks— Where in hell’s the ladder—”

Scorchy Langlie’s voice, jerky with gasping breath, rasped out above the rumble of boots on the floor overhead:

“The marshal’s croaked—I let him have a bash on the noggin an’ he got Ike’s slug through his hide. I ain’t so sure of Wade.”

Footsteps clattered dully, receding in murky distance.

Wade, scuttling along the cellar wall in gloom thick enough to handle, brought up short and froze, not daring to breathe, as he heard boots thudding closer to hand. The killers who had opened fire at the spot where he had landed were no doubt feeling about for his corpse.

Then a hoarse whisper:

“Let’s get out of here, Flannagan. Bret an’ Collier have made it by now.” There followed the sound of men climbing a ladder.

Wade got to his feet. He was alone in the cellar now, he felt. But what had happened?

Only a quarter of a minute ago, Bret Redfern and Black Bill Collier, handcuffed and sullen, had faced Judge Alamo Burkett in front of the bar which served as an altar of frontier justice. Then the dropping trapdoor had plunged the two prisoners into this moldy-smelling cellar.

Wade knew, even as his racing brain reviewed his pinched-off memory of events, that this had been planned carefully in advance by Redfern's henchman, as a last desperate resort to save their leader from the gallows.

"There's some way to get out of this cellar," thought Wade, groping his arms about in the darkness. "It's a cinch Redfern's cronies wouldn't trap themselves under a saloon this way if they didn't have a hole to crawl out of—"

From overhead came the sound of ax blows. Men were getting into action in a hurry, seeking to chop out the bar which held the trapdoor intact.

Satisfied that he was alone in the cellar, Wade fumbled for a match in his shirt pocket, scratched it into flame along the wing of his chaps.

His eyes raced over the scene exposed by the guttering match.

Rocky Donovan, writhing in agony, still lay on the pile of gunnysacks beneath the trapdoor. Blood was running thickly from a bullet hole in his back.

The original steps which had once led up to the trapdoor had been moved to one side. The cellar was unfurnished saved for a monstrous beer cask and a litter of whiskey bottles and débris on the floor.

Pandemonium ruled in the barroom overhead. Wade thought he heard Curly Joyce's soprano scream pealing out above the yells of men, the cursing of deputies seeking to chop through the floor.

Then wood split as ax bits cut through to the wooden bar which had locked the trapdoor from beneath.

A moment later the trap dropped, flooding the cellar with yellow lamplight, putting a slanting bar of illumination on the blood-soaked body of the dying marshal.

Men peered anxiously down into the cellar, guns in hand, yet none of them daring to leap into the opening for fear of meeting a riddling blast of lead from the outlaws who had whisked Bret Redfern and Collier away from the very brink of doom.

Cupping hands to mouth and remaining well back out of sight from the alert gun muzzles overhead, Hal Wade yelled:

"It's safe, men! Wade speaking! Redfern an' his skunk outfit have vamoosed. I don't know how, but they're not in this cellar now!"

Curly Joyce wriggled her way through the phalanx of men grouped about the six-foot-square opening in the barroom floor, lowered her boot-clad legs over the opening, then swung down and hung a moment to the floor beam, clinging by her fingers.

Then she released herself and dropped to the mattress of gunnysacks, peering wildly about as Hal Wade stepped forward.

"Hal! Hal!" she cried, rushing forward and

flinging herself against him. "I was sure—you'd be killed when—"

Wade pushed her aside and leaped to Rocky Donovan, turning the wounded marshal over.

There was an ugly welt on the marshal's skull, where Scorchy Langlie had struck him, probably with a bottle or some other weapon which the erstwhile defense lawyer had snatched to hand after leaping down into the pitlike basement.

Then men were jumping down into the cellar, most of them men with deputy marshal's badges pinned to their shirts. Judge Alamo Burkett allowed himself to be lowered by willing hands next, and pushed forward to confront Wade.

"What happened?" panted the judge, his face pale with the suddenness of events. "Having prisoners vanish in thin air—it's impossible—"

Wade, feeling the feeble pulse in Donovan's wrist, stood up and glanced about.

"Quick!" he yelled. "There's another way out of this cellar somewhere—we've got to find it. Otherwise Redfern will make his getaway for keeps."

Wade knelt to take the marshal's six-guns from their holsters.

Then, ignoring Curly Joyce's scream of protest, Wade shoved through the crowd of deputies and stared about at the four walls of the cellar.

A moment later he saw what he was looking for—an opening in the boarded-up walls, where planks had been ripped aside. There was a large pile of fresh dirt near the opening, and it told Wade what he had wanted to know.

Redfern's accomplices, working secretly, had somehow managed to sink a tunnel into the liquor-storage cellar beneath the barroom which had served as a courtroom for Redfern's murder trial.

Striking another match, Wade pushed his way through the opening in the cellar wall.

He was faced by a ladder. Looking up, he saw that the ladder led to the floor of the barroom outside the cellar's limits. Heavy sills had proved too much for Redfern's rescuers to saw through, without discovery, so they had crawled between the ground and the floor, sunk a small shaft to the level of the cellar's bottom, then had simply knocked out time-rotted planks to gain entry to the cellar.

Blowing out the match, Wade holstered one of the marshal's guns by jabbing it in the waistband of his chaps.

Then, gripping a cocked .45 in his right hand and climbing with the other, Wade made his way to the top of the short ladder.

A dozen feet away, through a forest of foundation blocks, he saw the light of dusk on an alleyway.

He saw, too, the gouged-out marks where Bret Redfern and his followers had wriggled, in snake fashion, under the saloon floor.

Excited deputies climbed up the ladder behind Wade as the cowboy made his way on his belly to the outer wall of the saloon.

He paused a moment, scanning the alleyway, knowing that Redfern might have left a guard to riddle him with slugs if he poked his head into view.

But the alleyway was deserted; boot marks showed where Redfern and his crew of owlhooters had made a hasty retreat toward vacant lots in the rear of the Silver Dollar Saloon.

Risking an ambush bullet, Hal Wade wriggled out from under the saloon and made his way down the alley, following the tangle of fresh bootprints.

The foot tracks ended at the rear end of the saloon; there, significantly enough, were the marks of steel-shod horses' hoofs.

Wade's eye swept the weed-grown lots and the ramshackle buildings which hemmed in the lots, but saw no trace of fleeing horsemen. Any one of a dozen trails led from the outskirts of the mining camp, into the upflung Badluck foothills which were fast turning black in the thickening twilight.

Shoving Donovan's other gun into the waistband of his chaps, Wade turned around to face four of Donovan's star-toting deputies who had followed him up out of the liquor cellar and had crawled under the saloon roof to the alley.

"No use, men," said Wade heavily. "You can hustle over to the Blue Skull Saloon, but you probably won't find Redfern. This was all planned out sometime this week. They were just waiting for Langlie to signal the men in the cellar below that Redfern or Collier, or both, were on the trapdoor. By now they are probably to hell and gone."

Yelling oaths, the deputies headed down the alley toward the main street. Piles of tin cans impeded their progress, and shutting off the alley from the street proper was a ten-foot board fence, which had shielded Redfern's getaway from the eyes of the crowd which jammed the street.

Wade crawled back into the saloon cellar and was dusting himself off when Curly Joyce forced her way through the throng which packed the cellar, halting at his side.

"Rocky's conscious—and calling for you, Hal," the girl cried in his ear. "He can't last long."

In desperate haste, the cowboy elbowed his way back to the pile of gunnysacks under the trapdoor.

Doc Phelps had been lowered into the cellar, and was on his knees beside the prostrate lawman. He shook his head as he glanced up and saw Wade beside him.

Recognition gleamed in Rocky Donovan's eyes as Wade bent over his face.

"I knew . . . I'd get it . . . some day—" he gasped, blood gurgling in his throat as he spoke. "Looks like . . . Redfern outthought us . . . Wade . . . even at the very last—"

The cowboy struggled to keep his voice from breaking:

"Your deputies are tailin' him now, Rocky. Redfern and Collier are wearin' your irons, remember. They can't get far."

The gray tide of advancing death was on Rocky Donovan's twitching countenance as his hand groped up to touch Wade's.

"You . . . carry on . . . son," the lawman wheezed. "One good thing . . . after this . . . Redfern won't dare . . . come back to Deadhorse—"

Wade inhaled deeply, trying to think of something to say. Curly Joyce was weeping softly behind him, unable to look at the dying countenance of the man who had backed her play consistently from the first.

"I'll promise you this, Donovan," panted Wade at last. "I'll dab my loop on Redfern—"

Donovan made a plucking motion at the marshal's star on his vest. Reading the lawman's thought, Wade unpinned it and placed it in the dying man's fingers.

Summoning his fast-ebbing strength, Rocky Donovan lifted the emblem of authority and affixed it to Hal Wade's shirt. Then his hand fell back, and before he could speak again Rocky Donovan had gone to join the other martyrs who had given their last full measure to bring law and order to a ruthless and benighted West.

—Chapter XXVII—

TERROR BY NIGHT

The next couple of hours were forever a tangled jumble in Hal Wade's memory.

The realization that Rocky Donovan had made him his successor to the marshal's office in the mining camp brought with it a sense of deep responsibility, not only to the rough pioneer community that had depended on Donovan for what semblance of law and order Deadhorse had boasted, but also the solemn promise he had given the lawman a moment before his pulse beats were numbered.

Doc Phelps, as official coroner for the district, took charge of Donovan's corpse, removing it from the cobwebby basement of the Silver Dollar Saloon and transferring it to a spare room in the jailhouse which served as a morgue.

Trailing Redfern, Collier and their rescuers was next to impossible, what with gathering night blotting out all traces of their getaway tracks.

Wade's first official act was to slap a padlock on the Blue Skull Saloon. Then, keeping to side streets to avoid the excited throngs who were discussing the fantastic last-minute escape of

Redfern and Collier, the Arizonan made his way to the Bonanza Hotel.

He found Paydirt Patterson visiting Curly Joyce and her father. Doc Phelps' arrival was timed with Wade's. The murder of Rocky Donovan hung over them like a pall, depressing them far more than had the escape of their enemies.

"I can't for the life of me figure things out—I'm still dazed about the whole affair," groaned Rex Joyce. "One minute the judge was sentencin' Redfern to stretch hemp. The next minute all hell had busted loose!"

Hal Wade seated himself on a leather-bound sofa between Doc Phelps and Curly Joyce, and stared moodily at the carpet.

"Redfern engineered the whole business as soon as he found out the trial was goin' to be held in that deserted saloon," responded the new marshal of Deadhorse town. "He slipped the word to Scorchy Langlie to get his men to dig down into that cellar.

"That big trapdoor that was in front of the bar—where the bartenders used to go down for liquor—was made to order for a getaway. Redfern knew when the time came for him to stand up and face sentence, he'd have to stand on that door. Langlie stomped his boot heel on the floor to signal his men waiting down below. That was all there was to it."

Doc Phelps shook his head despairingly.

"But to think that Langlie could heave both you an' Rocky into that trapdoor and jump down himself and get the door shut—before anybody could lift a finger—"

Wade sighed heavily.

"What's done is done," he said. "But the thing we got to think about is, what next? Will Redfern be content to stay out of Deadhorse and leave his saloon, his Lucky Lode mine, his stagecoach business? Or will he strike back?"

Paydirt Patterson pondered Hal Wade's question.

"Redfern's no coward. But he wouldn't dare show his neck around these parts again. Most likely he'll head for the border, and we'll never hear from him again. Judge Burkett will make some legal disposition of his property—and we'll all be able to breathe easy again."

Curly Joyce grinned ruefully. "I wish I could share your confidence that we've seen the last of Redfern," she said. "Personally, I don't think he will leave Nevada until he's had his revenge against the man who destroyed him and ran him out of Deadhorse. And that man is you, Hal."

The new marshal shrugged and stood up; Patterson and the doctor followed suit.

"I'll be in the saddle by daylight, and run down their tracks as far as I can follow 'em," Wade said. "I won't have any trouble getting a posse.

This town's plenty riled because Rocky Donovan was murdered."

They bade the Joyces good night, and Hal Wade made his way to the hotel room where he had so nearly been knifed to death prior to the trial.

He wished now that he had pressed charges of attempted murder on Scorchy Langlie; but he had not actually identified the old stage driver as his attacker that night. He had only the bowie knife with Langlie's initials on it for evidence.

Despite the crushing disappointment of Redfern's escape, and the personal sense of loss he felt in Rocky Donovan's death, Hal Wade went to bed and slept soundly.

In the bleak hours before dawn, Wade was roused from slumber by a frantic knocking on his door. He called out hoarsely even as he reached under his pillow for a Colt six-gun:

"What is it? Who's there?"

"Me—Curly. Get dressed quick, Hal—I'm afraid something terrible has happened!"

The panic in the girl's voice snapped Wade instantly awake. He leaped out of bed, dragging on his Levi's and cow boots.

Then, hastily buckling a single cartridge belt and holstered Peacemaker about his waist, Wade hurried to the door and opened it.

By the dim light of a kerosene lamp flickering on a wall bracket of the hotel corridor, he saw

Curly Joyce standing there, fear mirrored in her wide blue eyes, her copper-colored hair falling about her shoulders in confused array.

She had a Navaho blanket clasped about her, and had obviously been roused from sleep herself only a few moments before.

"What's wrong, Curly?"

She swallowed twice before answering, as if to control her voice.

"I'm not sure anything is, Hal. I just awoke with a sense of something being wrong—I can't explain it. Maybe it was a nightmare."

"That's understandable, considering the strain that trial put all of us to, Curly. I'll rustle up Doc Phelps an' bring you some sleepin' powders—"

She shook her head wildly.

"No—wait until I tell you. I got up and went across the hall to daddy's room. He snores terribly, and I think that's what awakened me—not hearing him snoring. Anyway, I listened at his door, and couldn't hear him even breathing. I tried to open the door—and it was locked. Bolted from the inside. He—daddy never locks his door."

The two strode down the hall and halted in front of Rex Joyce's bedroom. Wade was conscious of an uneasy prickle down his spine as he stared at the wooden panels of the door. What menace lay behind that barrier?

"Stand back, Curly. It's a flimsy door. We'll

bust in and set your fears to rest. I don't think anything's happened to your father, just because he's sleepin' quieter than usual."

Hal Wade stepped back, hardening the muscles of his shoulder as he lunged at the door.

The small sleeve bolt on the inside splintered from its screwed-down moorings under the force of Wade's lunge, and the door slammed wide.

Rex Joyce's room was silent. A gentle night breeze whipped the curtains of the wide-open window by his bed, but there was insufficient light from the outdoors to penetrate the shadows of the room.

Wade groped his way to the bureau, struck a match and lighted the kerosene lamp there.

A muffled scream came from Curly, still standing in the corridor doorway.

Joyce's bed was empty. Sheets and blankets were in a state of dishevelment.

And smeared on the pillow was a crimson stain, red in the lamplight!

Drawing his Colt, Hal Wade dropped to a squat to peer under the bed, his senses recoiling before the expected shock of seeing Rex Joyce's corpse tumbled to the floor. He saw nothing.

Then an odor of scorching wax reached Wade's nostrils and directed his attention to the hot chimney of the bureau lamp he had just lighted.

Something adhering to the glass chimney seized

Wade's attention, making him oblivious to the low moan of despair from Curly Joyce as the girl clung to the door casing for support.

There were words written on the lamp chimney —a message scrawled hastily over the glass with a tallow candle for pencil:

> Rex Joyce isn't dead. We're giving him three days to live. He will be turned loose if all charges against Redfern are dropped and everyone connected with the Boothill Express, including Hal Wade, get out of Nevada before the three days have ex—

Before Hal Wade could summon the presence of mind to blow out the hot flame inside the lamp, it was too late. The soft candle wax on the lamp chimney began to run and smoke, even as Wade read the scrawled words in feverish haste.

Before he could finish the kidnap message or see by whom it had been signed, the fateful words ran together in a mess of dripping tallow which in turn was converted into a wisp of rancid-smelling smoke before his staring eyes.

—Chapter XXVIII—

Blind Gamble

Wade went to Curly Joyce and took the trembling girl in his arms.

"Your dad wasn't murdered, Curly," he whispered. "Redfern acted quick—he knew where to strike and damage us the most. He just kidnaped your father."

The girl choked back her sobs as she heard Wade repeat the kidnap message from memory as best he could.

"In other words, sometime tonight Redfern or some of his gunnies went into your dad's room and knocked him out while he slept," explained Wade. "They wrote that kidnap note on the lamp chimney—plenty clever, because our evidence went up in smoke."

Curly disengaged herself from Wade's arms and looked up into the cowboy's eyes.

"I'm—finished, Wade," she whispered. "I've been bucking hopeless odds ever since—I tried running my Boothill Express in competition with Redfern. The day you got to town with that Rocking R cattle herd—when they tried to burn dad alive in our office—I was ready to give up then. You gave me the courage to keep trying. But now—I've got to give up."

Wade nodded grimly. He made his way to the window of Rex Joyce's room. Still leaning against the hotel wall was the ladder by which Joyce's kidnapers had made their entry into the Bonanza Hotel. They had probably lowered the old man's insensible body to the ground with a lariat.

Wade doubted if Redfern himself had engineered the kidnaping of Curly's father. But at any rate, Redfern had struck a stunning blow where it counted most. Curly Joyce might risk her own life to keep her Boothill Express coaches rolling—but she would not defy Redfern at the expense of her father's life.

"All right, Curly," whispered Wade, returning to the girl's side. "Come daylight, we'll post signs where Redfern's spies can see 'em, saying that Wells Fargo is folding up. We'll leave town—withdraw our charges against Redfern. With Donovan out of the picture and Patterson and Phelps agreeing not to buck Redfern, it'll be safe for him to come back to Deadhorse. It's our only chance to get your dad back alive."

Next morning, the startled citizens of Deadhorse gathered in front of the Wells Fargo Express office to read a placard tacked there before daylight by Curly Joyce, agent:

EFFECTIVE IMMEDIATELY,
WELLS FARGO EXPRESS CO.
IS DISCONTINUING ITS SERVICE
BETWEEN DEADHORSE AND
CARSON CITY, NEVADA.

The news of Rex Joyce's kidnapping was kept from the miners and townspeople, for Curly's genial old father was popular with the residents of Deadhorse.

Wade and Curly were agreed that it would not be a wise step to incense the populace of the gold diggings against Bret Redfern any more than was possible.

Getting Rex Joyce back alive from his captors depended on paving a clear path for Redfern to return to his outlaw kingdom in Deadhorse, and that would involve explaining the circumstances to Judge Alamo Burkett and getting that judge to promise, in the interests of Joyce's life, not to prosecute Redfern on the charges for which he had been found guilty.

Whip Gleason arrived in Deadhorse at noon with the incoming mail stage from Carson City. The oldster was dumfounded to learn that, during his absence, Wells Fargo had decided to withdraw its Boothill Express from the Washoe country forever.

Going to the Deadhorse post office for whatever mail might be addressed to Wells Fargo, Hal

Wade received an envelope which had been dropped in the letter box in Deadhorse the night before.

Its contents tied up with the mysterious kidnap note of the night before. Crudely printed to disguise the handwriting of its author, the note read:

> Rex Joyce will be held for three days. If at the end of that time all our requirements have been met, Joyce will be set free out on Bakeoven Desert where he can walk to Carson City. If Wells Fargo and Hal Wade refuse to clear Redfern and get out of Deadhorse, nobody but the wolves and buzzards will know what became of Joyce.

The letter was unsigned, but from the language in which it was couched Hal Wade was pretty sure that it had been composed by Black Bill Collier, who professed more of an education than Bret Redfern.

Wade carried the letter over to the Wells Fargo office, where Curly Joyce was busy packing up personal belongings in anticipation of a hasty departure the following day.

Tears of relief flooded the girl's eyes as she read the kidnapers' assurance that her father was still alive. She turned the page over, and there discovered something in shaky handwriting which Wade had overlooked on his first hasty reading of the letter:

Curly—Redfern means business. Do as he says.

Dad.

"That's his penmanship—it means he's alive!" cried the girl, hope springing afresh in her voice. "Oh, we must do as Redfern orders, Hal. I'll gladly surrender the field—leave Deadhorse and all I've lived and fought for so hard and long—I'll gladly surrender all that to get Dad back!"

Wade cast bitter eyes out through the office windows at the unkempt crowd of miners and townspeople who were congregated in front of the Wells Fargo shack.

Perhaps one of Bret Redfern's spies was reading that sign, watching their movements, this very moment—waiting to report to the outlaw, wherever he might be hiding.

As newly-appointed marshal, Wade knew he had legal authority to ride out to Redfern's Lucky Lode gold mine and search its maze of underground tunnels and shafts in his hunt for the fugitive killer.

But he knew his hands were tied. Once Redfern's spies reported to their hidden chief that Wade or Wells Fargo were not knuckling in to his demands, their prisoner, Rex Joyce, would be speedily killed, perhaps tortured.

Whip Gleason broke into Wade's thoughts as the wizened old jehu came stamping into the rear of the express office and jerked his head in a signal for the cowboy to come out back and talk to him.

"What's on your mind, Whip?" asked Wade dully, noticing the oldster's suppressed excitement.

"Listen, Hal—we ain't really givin' up the ship without a struggle, are we? All this packin' to leave town, and that sign about the Boothill Express foldin' up its tent—all that's bluff, ain't it?"

Wade shook his head soberly.

"I'm afraid not, Whip. Undoubtedly Redfern has spies planted in town to report on how we are reacting to his kidnap demand. After all, Rex's life is more important—to Curly, at least—than ridding Deadhorse of Bret Redfern."

Whip Gleason looked disappointed. He scrubbed his fringe of brown beard for a moment, then said:

"Looky here, son. I got a perty strong hunch I know who Redfern's spy will be—the hombre that'll leave Deadhorse an' contact Redfern."

"Who?"

"Pegleg Langlie. He's the broken-down old swamper who sprinkles sawdust on the floor of the Blue Skull Saloon and does odd jobs around Redfern's stable."

Wade's eyes slitted. He recalled having seen the wooden-legged old codger who polished spittoons in the Blue Skull Saloon.

"Pegleg Langlie— Any relation to Scorchy Langlie?"

"His brother. Don't forget that Scorchy's on the dodge as well as Redfern an' Collier. Sooner or later, I got a hunch, Pegleg will saddle up a cayuse and go off on a mysterious trip into the Badluck Mountains. The end of his trail will be where Redfern is hidin'—or I miss my guess. And wherever Redfern's holed up, we'll find Joyce being held."

Wade's eyes lighted for a moment with the possibilities contained in Whip Gleason's words. Then his shoulders slumped, and he shook his head.

"No dice, Whip. It'd be plump *bueno* if we could run down Redfern and smoke him and his skunk pardners out of their den. But if we tried it—an' Rex Joyce was dead when we found him—Curly'd never forgive me."

Whip Gleason turned on his heel and bow-legged off in the direction of the Silver Nugget stable to rub down his stage team.

Wade spent the rest of the day helping Curly Joyce make preparations for their departure.

Along toward sundown, a small posse of Rocky Donovan's deputies returned to town, having spent the daylight hours tracking Redfern.

The trail from the back of the Silver Dollar Saloon led off to the southward, to be lost finally in the trackless lava lands, the deputies reported.

"Donovan made you our new boss," one of the deputies spoke up, as they faced Hal Wade in the lobby of the Bonanza Hotel. "We're lookin' to you for orders from here on out, Wade. What do we do next?"

Wade inhaled deeply. He had been too busy during the day to remember that he was the new marshal of Deadhorse.

With an impulsive gesture, he reached up and unpinned the marshal's badge which Rocky Donovan had placed on his shirt a moment before his death. He handed it to the flabbergasted spokesman.

"I'm resignin' the job, Sanders!" the cowboy told the deputy.

Shocked looks faded into open derision among the tired, dust-covered posse riders. The man to whom Rocky Donovan had imparted his trust was letting them down in this hour of crisis, merely because Redfern's trail had petered out in the malpais.

"You got a yellow belly, Wade!" snarled Sanders. "We'll take that badge to Paydirt Patterson. He was Rocky's best friend. I reckon *he'll* wear that star—until he pegs Bret Redfern!"

Wade watched the men file out, a bitter smile on his face. He could not explain to them that his loyalty to Curly Joyce and her kidnaped father was forcing his hand tonight.

He headed upstairs, intending to go to his room for the night. A dusky figure waited for him in the hallway, and Wade's hand dropped instinctively to his gun butt until he recognized the waiting man as Whip Gleason.

"I got news, pardner!" whispered the old stage driver, his voice quivering with excitement. " 'Long about three o'clock this afternoon, Pegleg Langlie saddled up one of Redfern's hosses an' drifted out of town by one of the north trails, like he was goin' to the Lucky Lode or somethin'."

Wade waited for the oldster to continue.

"I was planted up on Pancake Ridge, where you an' me squatted with our field glass the mornin' before we wrecked the bridge an' got Patterson's bullion away from the Thunderbolt Express," Gleason went on. "I watched Langlie ride out of sight of the town. An' then, instead of keepin' on the Lucky Lode trail, Langlie heads off to the southeast."

Wade felt his pulse quicken with interest.

"There'll be a moon tonight, Hal," whispered Gleason. "I know I can pick up Pegleg's trail—I've prospected all through that country. Soft shale an' sand blows. It'll be easy trackin' Pegleg —and the end of his trail will be where Redfern's keepin' Rex Joyce. I'm dead certain positive my hunch is *bueno*!"

For a long moment, Hal Wade wrestled with inner feelings.

Perhaps Pegleg Langlie was leaving town merely on a prospecting jaunt. But what if he *was* Redfern's spy, with orders to observe what had happened that day in Deadhorse and ride out to Redfern's hideaway and report?

Failure to locate Redfern and rescue Joyce would mean final and complete defeat for Curly's Wells Fargo agency. But if they *could* rescue her father— Anyway, it was a blind gamble.

"We'll try it, Whip!" Wade said finally. "You have horses saddled and waiting up on Pancake Ridge. I'll meet you there an hour before moonrise. If we find out Pegleg Langlie's leadin' us on a wild goose chase, we can get back to town before mornin' without nobody being any the wiser."

—Chapter XXIX—

Trail to Nowhere

A slim sickle of lemon-rind moon cruised above the Badluck Range at midnight, covering Nevada with a ghostly witch-glow.

It found Hal Wade and Whip Gleason riding single-file through the brush-dotted ridges to the southeast of the mining camp, eyes raking the surrounding skylines frequently as they searched for traces of Pegleg Langlie's trail.

They had ridden from Pancake Ridge to the trail where Gleason had last seen Pegleg, before moon-up. Wade was positive his own departure on foot from the Bonanza Hotel had not been witnessed. So far as anyone in town—be it Curly Joyce or an unfriendly pair of spying eyes—could know, he was asleep in his hotel room.

"There's Langlie's sign!" whispered Gleason excitedly, as they were dipping into a shadowy ravine floored with alluvial sand. "See where he stopped to tighten up his latigo—see them deep marks where his wooden leg sunk in the sand? An' here's where he remounted, and rode off in that direction."

They spurred forward, following Pegleg Langlie's

trail through the twisting pit of the ravine. Moonlight outlined the tracks with light and shadow, making Langlie's trail easy to follow.

For two hours the hoof prints wound on and on through the badlands, rarely emerging from the bed of the dry creek it followed. In general, Langlie was traveling in a southeasterly direction, headed toward one of the most barren and sterile areas of central Nevada.

"It's a cinch there ain't any ore deposits in the direction he's headin'," grunted Whip Gleason, breaking the silence for the first time since they had spotted Langlie's sign. "That encourages me to think Langlie ain't out on no prospectin' trip, by grab— Besides, he wasn't carryin' no prospectin' supplies."

"Then he wasn't carrying food to Redfern and the others!" pointed out Wade. "Maybe he's just dusting out of the country—afraid a mob might string him up on account of what his brother did at the trial!"

Gleason had no reply to make to that point. They had already come too far to go back, now; and the fact that Pegleg Langlie was traveling so far without food supplies proved to both men that he must be heading for some place where it was.

If that place was Redfern's hideout, it was logical to suppose that the men who had enabled Redfern to escape from the courtroom cellar had previously stocked a hideout with food and ammunition.

The moon swung higher, as if to hold a lantern above the eroded buttes and box canyons along whose rim Pegleg Langlie's trail seemed to be winding, aimlessly, endlessly.

"Devil's Wigwam," grunted Whip Gleason, as they reined up their horses to rest briefly. The oldster was pointing toward a conical mountain of red volcanic stone due north of them, and toward which landmark Pegleg Langlie had veered. "Used to be a signal peak for Piutes an' Shoshones on the warpath. You can see the tip of it from Pancake Ridge, back of Deadhorse. If Redfern *was* hidin' on Devil's Wigwam, he could signal by flashin' a mirror in the sun, direct to Deadhorse."

They moved on, riding on either side of Langlie's trail. The moon, now, was a liability; it made the terrain stand out in brilliant relief, turning cactus stalks into human forms with the magic of shadow, making giant boulders resemble flimsy bushes and converting the fragile smoke-tree into seemingly granite blocks.

And then, as they reached the base of the Devil's Wigwam and started following Langlie's trail up its slope, Gleason and Wade halted up short as they saw the trail they were following suddenly join the tracks of several other horses, coming in from a different angle to the west.

“Seven hosses, so far as I can make out!” whispered Gleason, dismounting to inspect the sign with the painstaking care of a veteran frontiersman. “Langlie met ’em here, or else crossed this sign after seven other hosses had traveled it—”

Wade did some mental calculating.

“Redfern, Collier, Scorchy Langlie—the two men I know were down in the cellar waiting to rescue Redfern at the trial—one lookout probably posted out in the alley with their getaway horses—that’d make six men who hightailed it out of Deadhorse,” Wade reasoned. “One spare horse—maybe a pack mule. Gleason, our trail’s gettin’ hot.”

Their hunt given fresh impetus, the two pushed on into the dense chaparral of mesquite and manzanita, aspen and cactus forms which furred the conical base of the Devil’s Wigwam formation.

In the interests of prudence, the two dismounted and tied their horses in a piñon bosquet. Then, following the well-trampled trail leading in a spiral around the cone-shaped butte, Wade and Gleason headed off on foot, each with six-gun in hand.

The trail followed gentle ledges and mountain benches until they had left the south face of the Devil’s Wigwam and were on the sunrise side of the butte.

Suddenly Wade flung out a hand to halt Whip

Gleason, his eyes peering sharply to the northward.

Etched sharply against the star-powdered skyline was the unmistakable outline of a man-made structure, some hundred yards away—a shack, made of rocks.

"Looks like a prospector's shack," whispered Gleason, when his fading vision had finally picked up the cabin. "Plenty of 'em built around these parts where old sourdoughs lived before the Comstock rush drew 'em over into the Washoe country."

"The tracks we're following don't lead in the direction of that house," pointed out Wade, "but we can't pass it up without takin' a look-see. You wait here, Whip. I'll sneak up there and look the ground over."

Leaving Gleason waiting in the shelter of dense mesquite thickets, Hal Wade inspected his six-guns briefly, then headed off across the moon-drenched expanse.

The brush, struggling up the sterile lava slopes of the Devil's Wigwam, seemed to fatigue and thin out as the pitch increased its grade.

As a result, Hal Wade found himself forced to crawl on his belly up twisting dry coulees often so shallow as barely to hide him.

It took him the better part of an hour to traverse the three hundred feet of open ground between brushline and the stone shack.

“Got to come out in the open here,” Wade decided. “If there’s nobody in that shack, then all my precautions have been wasted. If there is—I’ll be a perty target in the moonlight.”

He unbuckled his spurs so that the Mexican rowels would make no betraying rattle. Then he crawled out of the shallow arroyo he had followed toward the cabin, and crept forward noiselessly until he had reached a corner of the stone house.

The wooden door of the shack had rotted away from its leather-strap hinges and had fallen outward, like a porch floor. There was a glass-less window at either end of the shack, and toward the nearest one Wade made his way.

Removing his sombrero so that its wide brim would not be too conspicuous against the moon-lit rectangle of the window, Wade peeped around the corner of the sill.

A shaft of moonlight fell through the open door of the cabin, to outline the figure of a man seated on a crude split-pole chair, his legs bound tightly to the chair legs with rope, his arms trussed behind the back of the chair. A bandanna had been tied about the prisoner’s mouth for a gag.

The man was Rex Joyce!

Wade stifled his quickened breathing and cocked an ear to listen. Rex Joyce was alive; Wade could see the slow lift and fall of his chest.

There was no guard in the cabin, either inside the door or out; Wade was positive of that. There was enough moonlight coming through door and windows to convince the cowboy that the room was deserted except for the helpless captive lashed to the chair.

To make sure that Redfern had not posted a guard at this remote cabin to keep watch over Joyce, Wade crept around the uphill wall of the cabin, turned the far corner and came up to the northeast front corner of the shack without seeing any sign of a guard.

Thus assured, the cowboy hurried to the doorway and stepped in, his sombreroed shadow falling across Rex Joyce and making the old man jerk erect in his bonds.

A wild light that Wade took for joy at his deliverance gleamed in the prisoner's eyes, and he made frantic inarticulate sounds with his throat, struggling against the gag.

"Don't worry, Rex!" said Hal Wade, jerking a pocketknife out of his chaps and opening the blade. "I'll have you out of there in a couple of ticks—"

Before cutting Joyce's bonds, Wade unknotted the blue bandanna which had been tied about the oldster's head.

Joyce spat out a wadded-up handkerchief which had been balled up and placed inside his mouth. His cry came in a gusty squawk that put terror in Wade's veins:

"Get out of here, Wade! You've stumbled into a trap!"

Before Wade could open his mouth to demand an explanation for Joyce's frantic yell, he heard a heavy wooden beam crack up in the attic.

Moonlight glinted on cartridge belts and buckles, as two men leaped down out of hiding to bar Wade from bolting out the open door.

With a yell, Wade recognized the crouched figures of Bret Redfern and Black Bill Collier, even as they landed on the earthen floor of the shack with heavy thuds.

"We knew you'd trail Pegleg here, Wade!" came Bret Redfern's voice, as harsh as clanking knife blades. "Get your arms up!"

Despair congealed the cowboy's veins. He stood transfixed beside Rex Joyce's chair, hands still held in the pose of getting ready to cut the old man's bonds. He stared at a double gun drop.

Before he could move a muscle, he heard grunts of exertion as a third hombre swung down out of the ceiling loft, where they had been hiding overhead, waiting for his arrival.

It was Scorchy Langlie, erstwhile driver of the Thunderbolt Express.

Doom had come, and Hal Wade knew it would be hopeless to whip a gun from leather and take Redfern with him into eternity. But instinct born of sheer despair made him plummet both hands to the lowslung butts of his Colt .45s.

Scorchy Langlie dived at him, outspread arms pinning his elbows to his side in the crushing fashion of a grizzly's hug. There was a gun in Redfern's hand, leveled at Wade's heart as the fugitive from Deadhorse justice charged in, Collier at his side. Redfern's gun roared like a cannon, at point-blank range.

Then Wade's head seemed to explode, and all went black—

—Chapter XXX—

Staked Out to Die

Daylight had come to the badlands when Hal Wade pulled himself back to consciousness.

He opened his eyes and stared about him, at first unable to remember where he was.

Then he recognized the heavy rock walls of the prospector's shack on Wigwam Butte. He was sitting on the earthen floor, arms bound behind his back, legs trussed at knee and ankle with rawhide. His shoulder blades were braced against a crude table built of peeled poles.

"Wade's comin' to," said a familiar voice off to one side. "Too bad Redfern's slug didn't bite a little deeper."

The Arizonan twisted his neck to one side, then froze with astonishment as he saw that he was sitting alongside Whip Gleason.

The veteran stage driver was likewise roped up, hand and foot, and propped against the shack wall.

Sight of Gleason, likewise a captive, destroyed the faint spark of hope which had burned in Wade's heart—the hope that Gleason had escaped capture and might be able to bring a rescue posse to the shack.

Directly in front of the two tied-up prisoners was Rex Joyce, still roped to the chair in which Wade had seen him. The old man was no longer gagged.

"Well, it looks like bad luck hatched out a batch of nits," commented Wade, grimacing as pain shot through his brain like hot blades. "How come you're here, Gleason?"

The oldster wagged his head solemnly.

"You an' me was a couple of damned fools, Hal," Gleason confessed. "The brush where you an' me first spotted this shack was thick with Redfern men, seemed like. You hadn't been gone ten minutes before two of his saloon gun hawks sneaked up on me an' bashed me with a rifle butt. I didn't even have a chance to yell a warnin' to you."

Rex Joyce smiled bitterly at the two men who had risked their lives—and stood to lose them—in a futile effort at rescuing him.

"Redfern himself spotted you fellers ridin' along Pegleg Langlie's trail a mile below the foot of Wigwam Butte," explained the old-timer. "He left his two gunnies down in the chaparral with others to ambush you. But when you separated, and Hal crawled up the slope alone, they just clumb up in the attic and waited."

Wade shook his throbbing head in an effort to clear it.

"Redfern creased your scalp with a slug,"

explained Joyce. "Soon as they had you out cold, Redfern yelled for his men to bring up Gleason. And that was that."

Despair put a nauseated sensation in the pit of Wade's stomach. He and Gleason had gambled everything and lost. And the fact that the three of them were still alive to greet the sunrise proved that Bret Redfern had some grim revenge in mind—a death that would be far worse than ambush bullets would have been.

"Where's Redfern an' Collier an' the others?" questioned Wade.

Before Gleason or Joyce could reply, Bret Redfern himself appeared in the doorway of the rock-walled shack.

Redfern's hairy wrists were no longer shackled with the handcuffs which he had been wearing at the time of his escape from the Deadhorse courtroom.

"My friend Wade is awake, eh?" chuckled the outlaw, hooking thumbs in gun belts as he stared at his trio of captives. "Well, amigos, you will not be kept in suspense as to what's going to happen to you."

Redfern turned and yelled outside:

" '*Sta bueno,* boys. Come and get 'em."

Wade felt a shiver coast down his spine at the menace in Redfern's tone.

A moment later, approaching footsteps heralded the arrival of the cadaverous Black Bill Collier, still wearing his black frock coat. Collier's manacles had likewise been removed from his wrists.

With Collier were the Langlie brothers, Scorchy and Pegleg, both in obviously high spirits.

"Drag our friends outside," ordered Redfern, his diamond-set teeth glittering in a triumphant grin. "We might as well dispose of 'em and be on our way to other parts. No use baking here in the desert."

Black Bill Collier proceeded to untie Rex Joyce from the chair, and seizing the old man by one armpit, dragged him out into the hot sunlight.

Scorchy Langlie followed, hauling Whip Gleason in similar fashion. Redfern hooked an arm under Hal Wade's right armpit and hauled him roughly through the doorway.

Down the hillside at the border of the chaparral, two sombreroed gunmen—the same pair, Wade knew, that had kidnaped Rex Joyce from his hotel room in Deadhorse and who had rescued Collier and Redfern from the courtroom in Deadhorse two days before—waited with a cavy of saddled horses, ready to leave as soon as the trio of captives had been "disposed of" according to Redfern's dictates.

"You three are going to have plenty of time to think things over," Redfern explained. "We'll postpone Mr. Joyce's departure, however, until I am sure that things are ready for me to return to Deadhorse as a free man."

Wade and Gleason were dragged down the hillside to a patch of soft ground bordering a weed-choked coulee. Collier, however, dragged Rex Joyce directly to the waiting horsemen and Wade saw the Blue Skull Saloon gunmen loading Curly's father aboard a waiting horse.

Thoughts milled in Wade's head. Was Redfern going to shoot his prisoners and leave their bodies here on the desolate slope of Wigwam Butte for the coyotes and buzzards to devour?

He was not kept in suspense long.

Reaching the area of soft, broken ground surrounded by crusted lava, Redfern and Langlie came to a stop.

Pegleg Langlie had followed, and for the first time Hal Wade saw that the one-legged hombre carried a load of kindling wood in his arms.

The end of each stick had been pointed and the other end notched, in a manner similar to a tent stake.

A low cry of horror came from Wade's lips as he read the meaning back of those notched sticks.

"He's going to stake us out on an ant hill to die, Whip!" cried the cowboy, shuddering in his bonds. "If you got an ounce of humanity in you, Redfern, you'll shoot us like you would a dog."

Bret Redfern knelt on one knee and picked up a notched stake. Using a heavy lava rock for a hammer, he drove the stake into the ground to a depth of twelve inches.

Pegleg Langlie, meanwhile, was cutting a lariat into two-foot lengths by means of a jackknife which Wade recognized as his own.

"Unfortunately," Redfern commented, "Wigwam Butte is too barren to sustain even an ant hill. But you're quite right in assuming you are going to be staked out, amigo. Staked out in the open—with plenty of time to think things over before the Nevada sun drives you both into raving, loco maniacs. And after that, maybe the zopilotes and desert wolves will come around to keep you company."

Wade bit his lips to keep from screaming out in horror and revulsion. Being spread-eagled and staked down in the pitiless desert sunlight was a torture almost on a par with being staked out on an ant heap.

With grim precision, Redfern went about his task of driving sharpened stakes into the ground in the form of a rectangle roughly approximating the dimensions of a coffin.

Then Pegleg Langlie severed the bonds which held Wade's arms helpless behind his back. The two men pulled out his arms to full length and then tied each wrist securely to a deep-driven wooden peg. Wade was too weak to offer resistance.

Wade's legs were then spread-eagled and

similarly tied to stakes placed three feet apart, ropes being tied securely to each ankle in such a fashion that it was impossible for the prisoner to lift a knee off the ground.

Five minutes later, and the two had completed their fiendish work on Whip Gleason. Then, as a final diabolical touch to their handiwork, stakes were driven close to their bodies, near their armpits. Longer ropes were bound over their ribs and tied to each of these stakes, thus impeding their breathing in the manner of a too-tightly cinched saddle girth.

"That'll hold 'em till the coyotes clean their bones," announced Redfern, rubbing his palms with satisfaction as he stared down at his helpless foemen. "Well, Wade, I guess this'll be adios. Ain't you goin' to tell me good-by an' wish me luck?"

Wade stifled a desire to cry out for mercy, knowing that to do so would only give Redfern further reason for gloating.

"Seein' the last of you won't be hard to take," grunted the cowboy, struggling to keep his voice casual, and not reveal the quaking horror within him. "You've raked in most of the pots since I set in on your game, Redfern. I admit I've been a mite curious about the way you won a few of them hands."

"Such as what?"

"Well, the time Whip and me brought Pedro

Merrick's carcass back to show Donovan, and prove it was a fake Indian raid that—"

Redfern threw back his head and guffawed loudly.

"That *was* fast work," Redfern admitted. "My boys dressed up as Injuns—Black Bill was with 'em that morning. They couldn't bring back Merrick's corpse without you fellers popping them from ambush. So, when they got back to Deadhorse and told me what had happened, I thought showdown had come."

Redfern chuckled at the memory.

"We went outside—and saw nobody around your Boothill Express," Redfern explained. "Pedro's body was inside. We had a real Piute Injun in the Blue Skull Saloon, playin' poker. I had the boys bring Pedro's body into the saloon. We buried him in the cellar. Then, while we were about it, the idea occurred to us to knock off this real Piute, and leave him in the stagecoach. It was all very simple—and worth the effort, seein' you and Rocky Donovan worryin' about it, wonderin' what had happened."

A hail from the waiting gun hawks down the slope made Redfern break off.

"Well, see you in hell, Wade. *Hasta la vista*!"

Desperation surged through Wade and Gleason as Redfern and his one-legged henchman strode off down the slope and mounted their waiting horses.

Wade, turning his head so that his cheek pressed against hot gravel, was able to see the outlaws ride off into the chaparral, Rex Joyce accompanying them on his own last ride.

Finally the sound of hoofbeats died on the fevered desert air, giving way to a silence broken only by the hoarse breathing of the doomed men.

"Looks like finish," panted Whip Gleason, jerking helplessly at the stakes which bound him. "Anyway—it's a honor to play out my string with an hombre like you, Wade. I reckon we both done it—for Curly's sake."

High in the brassy vault of the sky, vultures soared on motionless wings—circling harbingers of death.

—Chapter XXXI—

Smoke

Hours dragged. Sunlight drew the sweat from their bodies relentlessly, until skin grew too dry for perspiration glands to function. Then their torture became intense, unbearable.

At first they talked, in the manner of men sharing a death cell. They talked of anything, everything except the utter hopelessness of avoiding the slow death which Bret Redfern was meting out.

Nor did they mention the fear that was uppermost in their minds: the fear strong men admit and dread, the fear that their sanity would totter long before physical unconsciousness came to their aid, mercifully blacking out the effects of the blazing sun, the hot dry wind that rustled the brush in the coulee alongside their place of doom.

Bluebottle flies, coming from nowhere, buzzed intolerably.

Dry, stinging dust was whipped by vagrant breezes to clog their nostrils and eyelashes, chafe their skin.

Blisters began to appear in their flesh where

bonds too tightly drawn had cut into the skin at their wrists. Their feet were slowly swelling inside their boots.

Once, in midmorning some three hours after Redfern and his henchmen had disappeared, a flare of hope came to Hal Wade.

Both he and Gleason had wrenched savagely in their bonds, giving way to momentary panic, ceasing only when exhaustion paralyzed their muscles and told them the grim fact that it would be impossible to wrench free of the stakes which pegged them prostrate to earth.

That flare of hope came when Wade, struggling with the superhuman strength which desperation gives to dying men, managed to wrench his left arm stake free of its confining dirt.

But due to the rope which held his shoulders pinned to the ground, he was unable to use his free hand to wrench at other pegs. It was physically impossible to get at the stake driven alongside his left ribs and holding the rope that crossed his torso. The other pegs were far beyond his utmost reach.

He found himself wondering dully whether Redfern had not intentionally driven his left-wrist stake into loose soil so that he could uproot it, only to find further escape impossible.

At least he was able to fan his face, keep the annoyance of flies and other winged insects away from his eyes and mouth.

Whip Gleason's strength was fast ebbing, due to his advanced age. Wade knew that sunstroke, the overheating of blood in time-hardened arteries, would probably bring swift oblivion to the veteran stage driver many hours before sundown.

The sun reached the noon position in the sky and started down toward the west. But it would be four hours, at least, before the cool shadow of Wigwam Butte crept up over them, bringing respite from the sizzling heat.

Worse than the torture of swollen ankles and wrists under tightly-knotted bonds, worse than the pain which ate at his bullet-furrowed scalp, was the knowledge in Wade's mind that hope of rescue was futile.

No one knew that he and Gleason had come out into the badlands on their nocturnal mission. Wigwam Butte was in an area shunned by prospectors and beasts of prey, for it was without waterholes, without shade. Its barren terrain had been proven devoid of gold or silver lodes. There would be no chance prospectors coming by.

Finally, in a stupor of pain, Hal Wade's twitching left hand groped into the pocket of his shirt and drew out matches and makings. But in his present condition, he could not even enjoy the solace of a cigarette.

It was the soft whisper of the breeze in the tumbleweeds which filled the coulee nearby—a whisper as of a thousand tiny voices, jeering him with the prospects of their approaching doom—that put the seed of an idea in Wade's inflamed brain.

"Whip, I've got an idea!" called out the cowboy, twisting his head to stare at his fellow prisoner a few feet to his right. "I think maybe—"

He broke off, as he realized that Gleason was unconscious, that Gleason had fainted from overexposure to the sun's rays. For a moment a feeling of loneliness swept over Wade, as he wondered if the old man was dead. He hoped so. Yet— No, Whip Gleason's stanch old heart was still beating. Wade could see the steady, but ebbing pulse on the old man's reddened neck.

A few inches from Wade's body grew a stubby creosote brush whose roots had finally given up the futile search for water in the sterile soil and had died.

Wade struck one of the matches in his palsied hand, and ignited the creosote brush. It burst into flame, like a smoking torch alongside him.

Seizing the bush in his fist, Wade jerked it out by the roots and held it aloft, the fire scorching his fingers.

Then, with a desperate sidewise motion of his free arm, the cowboy threw the blazing scrub half a dozen feet to his left, saw it vanish into the low coulee.

Almost instantly, there was a crackling *whoosh* of sound as the blazing creosote set fire to the tumbleweeds and ignota brush which filled the tiny arroyo.

Thick smoke billowed up, as the weeds were consumed by a steady eating wall of flame.

A benevolent wind sweeping down the desolate slope of Wigwam Butte pushed the fire before it, gutting the tinder-dry weeds as the blaze worked steadily downhill.

Within fifteen minutes the fire had gone the length of the coulee and was breaking out in the heavier mesquite and smoke trees a hundred yards down the slope.

The roar of blazing chaparral was unheard in Wade's brain above the tom-tomming of the pulse in his eardrums. But he saw the tumbling columns of white smoke lifting up into the hot Nevada sky.

Soon the smoke, circling Wigwam Butte, had cut off the hot glare of the sun, bringing a certain relief to the staked-out prisoners below.

If Wade's idea netted nothing more, at least it would keep the spark of life in their bodies until sundown brought merciful coolness and possibly a dew to relieve the burning sensation in blotter-dry flesh.

Wade never knew when he drifted over the divide into unconsciousness. His senses were too dulled to note the diminishing thunder of his heart in his ears, too stupefied to register the fact that a merciful relaxation was loosening his knotted muscles. Finally he was swimming in a void of oblivion.

"They're O. K. They're both too damn tough to kill."

"Hand me that wet sack, Neeley. Bathe Gleason's head again, boys. He's worse off on account of his age."

"A sip of whiskey won't do Wade any harm. Lucky you brought your kit along, doc."

The words were so much meaningless confusion in Hal Wade's consciousness.

He felt the neck of a whiskey bottle being reamed between his lips, felt the fiery liquid going down his throat. He swallowed automatically, struggling to keep from letting the alcohol trickle down his windpipe.

Gentle fingers were massaging his wrists. His legs and feet felt oddly free; no longer were they confined in boot leather.

"Gleason's beginning to cuss. Won't he brag when he finds out he come to quicker than Hal?"

Then Hal Wade began recognizing the speakers by their voices. Doc Phelps, the Deadhorse medico, was giving the orders. A voice that belonged to Paydirt Patterson was somewhere in the back-ground.

Of course it was impossible. This was delirium, the thing Wade had dreaded. A mental mirage. Pretty soon he would be hearing the voice of his mother, twenty years dead. Or Curly Joyce's laughter—

He opened his eyes.

It was night. The air held a tang of wood smoke. Men with kindly grins on their faces were standing all about.

Firm, gentle hands helped Wade to a sitting position, supported him while he glanced about, still groggy.

His tongue no longer felt like a ball of cotton in his mouth. His ears no longer drummed like a—

"You're all right, Wade. So's Whip Gleason. We found the two of you just at sundown."

The cowboy focused his reeling vision on the kindly face of Zebediah Phelps, M.D.

"I don't savvy," whispered Wade, his voice a croak in his own hearing. "I don't . . . savvy—"

He rested another ten minutes before Phelps gave him another shot of reviving whiskey, and replaced the wet gunnysack which was wrapped about his throbbing head.

Then his brain was clear enough to understand the talk going on around him.

Whip Gleason was sitting nearby, gulping at a canteen.

Paydirt Patterson was helping hold Gleason in a sitting position. The badge that had belonged to Rocky Donovan, the marshal's star that Wade himself had worn briefly, gleamed in the starlight.

"You aren't dreaming, Hal," came Doc Phelps' assuring voice. "As soon as we found out you and Whip were missing this morning, we organized a posse to scour the hills for a trace of you."

Wade nodded, understanding at last. These men who had come out to Wigwam Butte to save them from a lingering torture were members of Marshal Paydirt Patterson's posse, then.

"How'd you . . . find us?"

The doctor grinned.

"We spotted a column of smoke over this direction," he said. "Don't ask me how that fire got started, but anyhow we figgered maybe it was a signal. We hightailed it over here—and damned if we didn't locate you and Whip, staked down to the dirt here. Redfern's work, or I'm loco!"

Wade sighed deeply. His scheme had been a success. His desperate plan of starting a brush fire and bringing succor had worked, fantastic and impossible though it had seemed in his own head.

"Yes. We figgered to find where Rex Joyce was bein' kept prisoner—and stumbled in a trap that Collier and Redfern had set," answered Hal Wade.

"Where's old Rex now?" asked Paydirt Patterson anxiously.

Wade shook his head.

"*Quién sabe*? He's still a prisoner of Redfern's."

A moody silence overcome the hitherto exultant posse who had saved the lives of Redfern's victims. At the showdown, Redfern still held the winning ace—in his third prisoner, Rex Joyce.

In all probability, Rex Joyce would lose his life as a result of last night's abortive attempt to save the kidnaped oldster, in direct defiance to Redfern's ultimatum.

Such an event, Hal Wade realized with a sinking sensation, would destroy forever whatever feeling Curly Joyce had for him. Regardless of his good intention—regardless of the fact that he and Gleason both had been willing to lay down their lives to restore old Rex to his daughter—Wade knew that in running contrary to Redfern's kidnap demands, he would never stand forgiven for Joyce's murder, in Curly's viewpoint.

—Chapter XXXII—

End of the Boothill Express

It was noon on the following day that Paydirt Patterson's posse returned to Deadhorse town, bringing with them the two missing men they had set out to find.

Doc Phelps had ridden to town an hour in advance of their arrival. The wise old medico had guessed the cause for Wade's dejection, and accordingly had sought out Curly Joyce at the Bonanza Hotel and laid his cards on the table.

Thus it was, when the Arizona cowboy entered the lobby of the Bonanza and saw Curly Joyce waiting for him beside a corner window where they had talked on previous occasions, that the girl was able to muster up a smile to help put Wade at ease.

"Curly, I've got—something to tell you that'll tear your heart out," the cowboy began. Then words balked. He had carefully rehearsed what he was going to say to her, many times on the ride in from Wigwam Butte.

But now, realizing that what he had to tell her would sever her friendship for him for all time, he was at a loss to speak.

Curly Joyce, her eyes brimming with sudden tears, reached out a small bronzed hand to touch the cowboy's arm.

"I know what's bothering you—Doc Phelps explained everything," she whispered.

Wade looked up, his face taut with strain.

"You mean—you know me an' Gleason tried to—to bring your father back?"

"Yes, Hal. You shouldn't have defied Redfern, knowing he would kill my father if he thought we were not acceding to his demands. But—"

Wade's jaw muscles gritted in an agony of despair.

"I know. I've just as good as—signed your dad's death warrant. You ought to unsling that six-gun of yours and fill my hide full of holes, Curly."

The girl shook her head.

"No. You . . . you meant everything for the best. I . . . I doubt if Redfern would have spared dad's life anyway. He would have double-crossed us—sent dad back—dead."

Wade said nothing. He, likewise, had never trusted Redfern's offer to spare Rex Joyce's life on the condition that Wells Fargo would pull up stakes and leave Deadhorse forever. Otherwise he would never have made the final desperate attempt to trace the old man's kidnapers.

"Hal." He looked up, to see that Curly Joyce was smiling. "Hal, you . . . you're all I've got now. I almost lost you—yesterday. That would have been—more than I could have borne."

Wade straightened, as if the weight of the world had rolled off his shoulders with her words. Before he could speak, an interruption came in the form of Paydirt Patterson. The new marshal came into the hotel lobby with a prisoner—a bewhiskered old desert rat with a wooden leg buckled to his stump of a knee.

"Look who was waitin' for me at the jail house, Wade!" called out the owner of the Red Eagle mine.

Wade stared incredulously at Patterson's prisoner. It was Pegleg Langlie, the selfsame hombre who the day before had helped stake Wade and Gleason out on the torrid slopes of Wigwam Butte to die!

Langlie displayed no surprise on seeing Wade alive. He merely exposed tobacco-stained teeth in a confident leer.

"You buskies won't hold me for long," sneered the brother of the fugitive Scorchy Langlie. "You think I'd have come to town if I'd thought I'd git strung up? Not any."

Wade shot a quick look toward Patterson.

"He talks like he's holding a royal flush, Paydirt," grunted the Arizonan.

Pegleg Langlie glanced around the room to make sure he was not overheard. Then, fixing his faded eyes on Curly Joyce, the outlaw said acidly:

"Curly Joyce, here, will see to it I'm turned loose. If she plays her cards right, she stands to see her old man again, alive an' kickin'."

Wade's heart leaped with new hope at Langlie's words. It seemed incredible that Bret Redfern was still willing to dicker with the Wells Fargo agent for the return of her kidnaped father; incredible that Redfern would not double-cross her, once he was in possession of his freedom again.

"Go on, Pegleg," whispered the girl. "What did you come here for?"

Langlie shook his arm free of Patterson's grip.

"Redfern wants me to bring him a legal writ, or somethin' from Judge Burkett, declarin' a mistrial an' absolvin' Redfern from any guilt in the matter of Sam Smith's murder."

Curly Joyce nodded eagerly.

"The judge has already given me that paper," she said. "Only yesterday. He said his only legal excuse for doing such a thing was in view of the fact that the evidence against Redfern was purely circumstantial."

Pegleg Langlie grinned triumphantly.

"I'm likewise to bring back the marshal's badge that Rocky Donovan used to wear," said the one-legged hombre, with a significant sidelong glance at the nickel-plated star on Patterson's vest. "That's in token that there won't be any lawman waitin' here in Deadhorse to clap Redfern or Collier or my brother in jail."

With a savage oath, Paydirt Patterson jerked off the marshal's badge and shoved it into Langlie's hand.

"For Rex Joyce's life, I'll do it!" snarled the miner. "What else does Redfern expect?"

Langlie shrugged.

"Curly knows what Redfern expects. He wants the Boothill Express to move out for good. He says there ain't room in Deadhorse for Wells Fargo an' him."

Hal Wade re-entered the conversation with the query he knew Curly Joyce did not have the courage to ask:

"All right—you can tell Redfern that Wells Fargo will be moved out of Deadhorse by this time tomorrow. We're doing our part—canceling the charges of murder against Redfern, the marshal's resigned his job, and the Boothill Express is surrendering. What guarantee have we got that Curly's father will not be murdered in cold blood as soon as Redfern knows the coast is clear for him to return to town?"

Pegleg Langlie's next words had the ring of sincerity, in spite of the distrust of his listeners:

"Redfern ain't a fool. He'll keep his side of the bargain—otherwise he'd have murdered Joyce yesterday at Wigwam Butte. I got proof with me that Joyce is still O. K."

Reaching in his pocket, Langlie pulled out a

crumpled piece of paper. He handed it to Curly Joyce, who read aloud:

"Curly dearest:

"I am still all right. As soon as you folks have done your part, I will be put on a horse somewhere out in the Bakeoven Desert, and will meet you in the Goldrush Hotel at Carson City. We got everything to gain and nothing to lose by trusting Redfern. I beg you not to make another attempt to save me or to tryand follow Pegleg Langlie to where I am being kept prisoner. Next time I would be killed for sure.

"Your loving father,
Rex Joyce."

Curly Joyce hugged the message to her heart, and turned to Hal Wade with real joy shining in her eyes.

"Hal, I'm satisfied. The end of the Boothill Express means nothing to me now. All I want is to get dad back—safe."

Langlie smirked insolently, cocksure of his safety here in the midst of his enemies. After all, he held all the aces in the deck.

"The judge's release of charges against Redfern and Collier is in the hotel safe, yonder," said the girl. "And I give you my word that no one will try and trail you when you leave, Pegleg."

A few minutes later Curly Joyce handed the leering prospector an official-looking envelope sealed with wax and containing the documents which would guarantee Bret Redfern and his henchmen freedom from molestation of the law when they saw fit to come out of hiding.

As Langlie turned to go, Hal Wade said:

"Pegleg, you tell your sidewindin' boss that he can turn Joyce lose *mañana.* Come daylight tomorrow, the two Boothill Express stages will be pulling out of Deadhorse for the last time. I'll be driving one, and Whip Gleason the other."

The one-legged hombre grinned triumphantly.

"I'll tell him, Wade."

The cowboy's jaw squared grimly as he seized Langlie by the arm.

"And tell him this for me, too, Pegleg. Tell Redfern that if Rex Joyce ain't at the Goldrush Hotel in Carson City like he promised, by tomorrow night, that I'll hunt Redfern down and fill him with slugs if I have to spend the rest of my life hunting him."

Langlie nodded.

"I'll tell him, Wade," he said.

Wade's eyes blazed with baffled anger as he saw Langlie hobble out the door and head for the Blue Skull Saloon, in front of which his horse was waiting at the hitch rack.

—Chapter XXXIII—

Double-Cross Plans

Deep in the murky recesses of the Lucky Lode gold mine, at the far end of a tunnel that had followed a vein of yellow treasure till it petered out on a basalt fault, Bret Redfern sat on a powder box and stared moodily at a poker hand he had just drawn.

The ace of clubs, the ace of spades, and the two black eights. Even the fifth card was a black jack.

He was playing draw poker with Collier, Scorchy Langlie and his two gun-hung body-guards from the Blue Skull Saloon, using a flat slab of basalt in lieu of a table, by the flickering light of a coal-oil lantern.

Black Bill Collier, noting the sudden burst of sweat which oozed from Redfern's pores, grunted impatiently:

"What's eatin' you, Bret? I never seen your hands shake before. You got a better poker face than that, I hope."

Redfern slammed the hand down for them to see. Collier's bantering expression faded and his voice was a tense whisper as he said:

"Black aces an' eights! The dead man's hand!"

Redfern collected himself with an oath.

"This hidin' out is breakin' my nerve, boys," he panted, wiping perspiration from his face. "I ain't superstitious. But it gave me a jolt, drawin' that dead man's hand. I wonder if Pegleg's run into bad luck in town? Why ain't he back?"

The outlaw boss got to his feet and paced up and down along the timber-braced mine tunnel.

A few feet away, at the edge of the lantern light, Rex Joyce was seated on a bedroll. The old man's wrists were still knotted together.

They had come to Redfern's gold mine directly from Wigwam Butte the day before. The mine had numerous secret exits besides the main entrance shaft, and the part of the mine in which they were now hiding was blocked off from the other tunnels by wooden bulkheads, inasmuch as it was no longer productive.

Thus it was that none of Redfern's crew of miners, hauling ore to the crusher above ground, had any idea that their fugitive employer was hiding underground near at hand.

"Don't let a hand of cards booger you, chief," advised Scorchy Langlie. "Jest because Wild Bill Hickok drawed that same hand in Deadwood when he was shot in the back—hell! Suppose Hickok had drawed a royal flush? Would that mean it was an unlucky hand for a man to h—"

A winking eye of yellow light, far down the

tunnel, made Langlie break off his discourse. The outlaws jerked nervously erect, hands stealing to gun butts.

They knew that the other end of that tunnel was effectively hidden inside a box canyon, screened by brush, and virtually impossible for an outsider to locate.

Besides, one of Redfern's most trusted gunmen, whose idea it had been to kidnap Rex Joyce from his hotel room and thus defeat Hal Wade and the Boothill Express, was standing guard at the exit to the tunnel.

"It's my brother!" panted Scorchy Langlie. "I can tell by his hobbly gait as he carries that lantern."

Redfern relaxed, flexing his finger muscles to rid his hands of the palsy that threatened them. The suspense of waiting underground was telling on the man's iron nerves.

Within the minute, Pegleg Langlie arrived at the end of the cavern which they had selected for their hideout because of the availability of fresh water in a seepage nearby.

"I got good news, boss!" announced the one-legged outlaw. "Here's Judge Burkett's O. K. on you goin' free. And the Boothill Express will be closin' out by daylight tomorrow. I got Hal Wade's promise on that."

"Hal—*Wade?*"

Redfern's exclamation sounded like the bark of

an animal, in the shocked silence following Pegleg's announcement.

The one-legged prospector nodded, enjoying the surprise he had given the bayed fugitives.

"Yep. Hal Wade's got more lives than a damned cat. He was alive an' grinnin' when I had my showdown with Patterson an' Curly Joyce."

Redfern passed a shaking hand over his eyes.

"It's impossible!" he husked out.

Pegleg Langlie handed over the judge's document, which the kingpin outlaw accepted without visible enthusiasm. The news of Hal Wade's escape from Wigwam Butte was like a punch to the solar plexus.

"It wasn't Wade's ghost I seen," countered Langlie. "I didn't ask 'em for details, but from what I could see, Paydirt Patterson took a posse out into the hills and rescued Wade an' the old jehu, Gleason."

A chuckle of suppressed laughter from Rex Joyce made Redfern turn on their prisoner and unloose a tirade of profanity. When his passion had spent itself, Redfern ripped open Judge Burkett's envelope and scanned the document therein by lantern light.

"Looks *bueno*," he grunted, rubbing his stubbled jaw thoughtfully. "What else did you find out, Pegleg?"

The one-legged miner seated himself on an

empty powder box and went into a full description of his visit to Deadhorse that morning. Gradually Redfern began to relax, as confidence restored itself.

"The last thing Hal Wade told me," finished up Langlie, "was that if you didn't live up to your side of the bargain and get Rex Joyce safe to Carson City, he'd have a smoke-out showdown with you, come hell or high water. An' he meant it, boss."

Redfern's fists opened and closed. A dangerous light kindled in his eyes as he stared thoughtfully off into the darkness.

Then he whirled, to confront his men, their faces slick and shiny with sweat in the lemon-colored lantern glow.

"Boys, we stand to rake in the pot. We got the Wells Fargo outfit under our heels. But as long as Hal Wade is above ground, my fight ain't finished. I'm acceptin' Wade's challenge!"

Black Bill Collier scratched his lantern jaw thoughtfully. He respected Redfern's keen judgment and undenied courage. But now, he believed that his owlhoot leader was overplaying his hand, taking a useless gamble.

"Don't forget, Bret, you got more than your own hide to think about. If we don't turn Joyce over to his daughter alive and in reasonable good shape, we'll have Patterson to fight and gosh knows how many depities. The thing for you to do is forget your ruckus with Hal Wade. He'll leave Nevada if you don't hooraw him into fightin'."

Rex Joyce, knowing his own fate hung in the balance, realizing his life and his daughter's happiness depended on the outcome of Redfern's verbal clash with his men, leaned forward anxiously as he saw Redfern's evil face go bleak in the lantern light.

"You say Wade will be drivin' one of those Boothill Express tomorrow mornin', on the way of the mountains?" said Redfern, his gaze on Pegleg Langlie.

"That's right."

Redfern snapped his fingers, and his diamond-set teeth were exposed in a grin of exultation.

"Then Wade will never get out of the Badlucks alive. You know how he wrecked that Death River bridge an' dumped your mud wagon in the river that time, Scorchy? Well, that stunt of Wade's has given me an idea. Collier, you an' Scorchy are comin' with me. We're gettin' out of this rat hole an' gettin' into action."

Snatching up his black sombrero and the lantern which the sentry had given Pegleg Langlie, Redfern strode off down the mine tunnel.

Black Bill Collier and Scorchy Langlie followed, scowling with worry.

The mine tunnel curved off and away toward the right. Daylight glimmered in a faint speck at the end of a branch tunnel.

Five minutes' climb up the sloping cavern brought them to where Redfern's armed sentry guarded the secret exit from the Lucky Lode diggings.

"Flannagan," said Redfern crisply to his lookout man, "you rattle your hocks over to the powder house in the gulch, and load a case of dynamite and half a dozen boxes of detonator caps onto a mule, and bring along two shovels and a pickax. Got that?"

Flannagan repeated the order in a mumbling voice.

"Head out through Hawkeye Gulch as soon as it gets dark," continued Redfern. "Cross the divide and hide on top of Shoshone Peak, out where Bakeoven Desert meets the foothills of the Badlucks. You got that straight?"

Flannagan nodded.

"You can get there by midnight. Collier and me will be waiting for you there." Redfern paused, lost in thought. Then he said. "Flannagan, you go back and tell Pegleg to bring Rex Joyce over to Shoshone Peak tonight—make sure he isn't seen by any of our men or anybody else, because there may be a reward out for anybody who can corral Joyce and bring him to Deadhorse."

"I got you, boss," said Flannagan.

Redfern ducked through the narrow opening of the cavern and pushed his way through a dense jungle of chokeberry brush which grew inside the blind canyon which served as the secret outlet to Redfern's hideout.

Stabled in a natural cavern under the beetling granite cliffs were the outlaws' horses. Moving with feverish haste, Bret Redfern saddled up a powerful roan mustang, while Black Bill Collier did likewise with a sorrel gelding.

"What crazy idea you got in your noggin, boss?" demanded Scorchy Langlie, saddling his own mount. "Don't forget you're a hunted man—|we're all hunted men, maybe with bounties posted on our topknots, dead or alive."

Black Bill Collier, who rarely crossed his chief, grunted testily:

"I don't like this sashayin' around in broad daylight, Bret. You owe it to us to tell us what you're planning to do."

Redfern's eyes glittered with a fanatical light.

"If Hal Wade is goin' to drive a Boothill Express coach to Carson City tomorrow," said the outlaw, "he'll have to take the road that leads past Shoshone Peak. You know where that is."

Collier and Scorchy nodded. Shoshone Peak was the site of their fake Indian attack on the Wells Fargo stagecoach, in which Patterson's gold shipment had been seized and Pedro Merrick had been slain.

"Well, we're going to dig a hole between the

ruts there where the road is sandy," Redfern explained, as the three spurred on out of the canyon. "We're going to bury that box of dynamite that Flannagan will bring out on the mule tonight. On top of the dynamite will be a box of high-explosive caps. And covering all that will be a one-inch layer of sand."

Collier's brow drew into a network of lines as he tried to puzzle out what Redfern was driving at.

"I'm going to blow Hal Wade and his Boothill Express to hell," snarled Bret Redfern. "And I'm going to lay that trap so well that there won't be a chance of failure. You boys are going to help me."

—Chapter XXXIV—

Dynamite Trap

A tardy moon illuminated the bleak reaches of Bakeoven Desert shortly after midnight.

Unseen in the darkness that had shrouded the Badluck Mountains, several trails had led toward the bushy cinder cone known as Shoshone Peak.

Collier, Scorchy Langlie, and Bret Redfern had arrived at the designated landmark first; they had come by a lengthy, roundabout route, in order to make sure they were not spotted by hostile eyes.

Shortly before midnight, the gunman, Flannagan, plodded to the base of the cinder cone with a mule from the Lucky Lode stables. On the mule was packed a box of dynamite sticks, a carton of percussion caps, two hickory-handled miner's shovels, and a pickax.

A few minutes after Flannagan's arrival at the rendezvous, two more horsemen loomed out of the night. They were Pegleg Langlie and his prisoner, Rex Joyce.

The old Wells Fargo man was conducted to the summit of Shoshone Peak. There he was to behold a strange sight.

Bret Redfern, in the two hours he had awaited

the arrival of his men, had carried out the preliminary part of building his ingenious murder trap.

A .30-30 Winchester rifle had been set in the notch of a cleft rock on the summit of the cinder cone, its sights lined up on the faintly-discernible ribbon of the Deadhorse-Carson City stagecoach road on the desert flats below.

The rifle had been tied to the split boulder by means of lariats connected to its barrel and walnut stock, and further wedged into place with smaller stones.

"Pegleg, when you hear me whistle, I want you to pull the trigger of this gun," ordered Redfern. "We know it's aimed at the stagecoach road, but I got to know exactly where the bullet will land."

A few minutes later, Langlie was left alone with Rex Joyce, squatting beside Redfern's mysterious rifle set-up.

The moon bathed the desert with light by the time Bret Redfern and his henchmen, leading Flannagan's dynamite-laden mule, had reached the stagecoach road.

"Stand back, and everybody keep their eyes peeled to see where that bullet hits," ordered Redfern. "All right—"

The outlaw put fingers to lips and blew a short, piercing blast as a signal to Pegleg Langlie, waiting up on Shoshone Peak.

A few seconds later a flash of light came from the tied-down rifle on the cinder cone.

Instantly, a tiny geyser of alkali dust was kicked up by the .30-30 bullet as it hit the sandy roadbed.

The distant crash of the rifle was echoing over the desert as Bret Redfern leaped forward, to stick a small twig on the exact spot where the high-calibered slug had buried itself between the stagecoach ruts.

"That's where we bury the box of dynamite, boys," panted Redfern excitedly. "Flannagan, spread out the tarpaulin you got your pack wrapped in, so we can carry off the dirt we dig out of the hole. We can't take any chances of Hal Wade spottin' our trap when he comes along here in the morning."

The next half hour was filled with feverish activity.

Working silently, Redfern and Black Bill Collier dug a hole in the soft sand, using the shovels which Flannagan had brought from the Lucky Lode mine. The pickax was used to break hardpan into clods.

That done, Scorchy Langlie and Flannagan lowered the box of dynamite into the hole, moving gingerly as they fitted the case of high explosive into place.

On top of the box of dynamite, exactly under the spot where the bullet from the vise-locked rifle had struck, was placed the carton of percussion caps.

Then, on top of everything, was carefully placed a shallow layer of the original alkali dust which they had dug up.

While Collier and Flannagan were carrying away the tarpaulin with its load of extra dirt, to be dumped in a rock heap a hundred yards away from the stagecoach road, Redfern was fanning his wide-brimmed sombrero over the sandy road to obliterate any signs of digging and any telltale footprints.

"*Bueno*," panted Redfern, when the task was finished to his satisfaction. "I don't reckon an Apache Injun could ever tell anything had been planted under that road, let alone Hal Wade seein' anything from the top of a jouncin' stagecoach."

A half hour later, all plans for the morrow's death trap were complete. Their horses were cached in a gully on the north side of Shoshone Peak, out of sight from the two Wells Fargo stages which were due to pass that way within a few hours.

The wedge-held .30-30 rifle, its sights inexorably lined up on the roadway below so that its next bullet would explode the buried dynamite, was carefully recocked.

Only then did Rex Joyce break down, his stoic silence giving way to a hysterical sob:

"Redfern, kill me an' get it over with. Do anything with me—but don't carry out this idea of blastin' Hal Wade to hell. Maybe . . . maybe my girl Curly will be ridin' on that Concord along with Wade—ten chances to one she will."

Redfern guffawed callously.

"That ain't my responsibility, Joyce. But what you worryin' about? You ain't goin' to see your daughter again anyhow. Once Hal Wade's out of the way, I ain't worryin' about fulfillin' my side of this bargain."

—Chapter XXXV—

The Explosion

Two Concord stagecoaches, were drawn up in front of the Wells Fargo office on the main street of Deadhorse town as the dawn's slanting rays cut down through the mine-burrowed walls of Death River Canyon.

A crowd was on hand, despite the earliness of the hour; a crowd that was notable for its lack of exuberance, for the air of depression that sobered every face.

The older eyes in the motley audience grouped about the high-wheeled Concord knew they were witnessing the end of an era in the turbulent history of Deadhorse. Wells Fargo had become a part and parcel of the untamed West, and never before had the proud old express company struck its colors and retired in defeat from any field along the frontier.

Every man in that silent throng in front of the false-fronted shack that had once been Jimmy O'Niel's newspaper shop, sensed the undercurrent of drama that was responsible for Curly Joyce having pulled stakes.

As red-blooded Westerners with a sense of

innate justice, they resented the fact that the red-haired, hard-fighting girl had at last played out her string against bitter odds. Yet each man knew the menace that had forced her to surrender, the sinister monopoly which Bret Redfern and his gun-fanged wolf pack held over the destiny of the mining camp.

Paydirt Patterson, his marshal's star conspicuous for its absence, was the last to step up and shake Hal Wade's hand as the Arizona cowboy assisted Curly Joyce up the front wheel of the lead stagecoach.

"Hal, don't git the idea you're leaving this camp like a yaller dog with your tail tucked between your laigs," said the grizzled old owner of the Red Eagle mine. "If this was a man-to-man affair, you'd fight Redfern to the last bloody ditch, an' go down fightin'. But with a girl involved—"

Wade smiled bitterly. He had learned to love the bleak Nevada hills that hemmed in this rough mining camp; he hated to pull out and leave its rutted streets, its shabby buildings and canyon walls towering above the gorge of Death River.

But the play had been taken out of his hands by Redfern's master stroke of kidnaping Rex Joyce. Until Curly's father was restored to her, there could be no thought of retribution against Redfern or his lawless element. But it was bitter gall, having to leave the town like so much carrion for the Blue Skull Saloon wolf pack to devour.

"*Hasta luego*, Paydirt," grinned Wade. "Reckon my old job on the Rocking R cattle syndicate will be waitin' for me in Arizona. I'm—sort of hoping—maybe Curly will take up cattle business an' maybe forget her Boothill Expresses."

Wade went around to the other side of the stage and swung up into the driver's seat, picking up the lines and settling himself beside Curly Joyce.

He twisted in the seat to wave at Whip Gleason. The old-timer was holding his restive six-horse span in check with less than his accustomed vigor, but that was natural in view of the ordeal he had been through on Wigwam Butte—a grueling torture that would have meant the finish of many men half Gleason's age.

"Ready to roll, Whip?" called Wade. "Let's move!"

Whips popped and wheels rattled, as the two Concords rolled out of town by way of Redfern's erstwhile toll bridge over Death River.

The stages were loaded with personal belongings owned by Curly Joyce and her father, so that the teams had to toil up the heavy grade leading out of the Badlucks.

"I still wish you'd ride inside, Curly!" implored the cowboy, looking appealingly at the set-faced girl at his side. “I’m not expectin’ Redfern’s outfit to try and ambush us, seein’ as how we’re clearin’ out accordin’ to his orders. But just the same—it’s risky business, ridin’ out in plain view.”

Curly inhaled deeply and flung coppery hair back out of her eyes. Her heart was too full, too torn with emotions this black day of reckoning, for her to argue.

“Hal, the least I can do—for my own sake—is ride out of here with my head up, aboard my own stagecoach.”

The teams jogged on, dust rising in stifling smudge as hours ticked by. Up grade and down, skirting the perilous rimrock of Death River, crossing the new log bridge which had replaced the one destroyed by Wade and Whip Gleason, the retreating, defeated Boothill Expresses wound their way toward the level expanse of Bakeoven Desert, lying between them and their destination at Carson City.

By eleven o’clock they had traversed most of the rough country between them and Deadhorse, and were climbing the last steep grade which would take them over the foothills and down into Bakeoven Desert.

It was a glint of sunlight on polished metal, behind a mesquite bosquet midway up the barren slope, that warned Hal Wade that a possible ambusher was hiding behind that dot of scrub brush a thousand yards ahead.

Wade hauled back the reins to stop the team, and set the brake lever. He moved unhurriedly, as if giving the horses a chance to regain their breath before tackling the rest of the long pull.

"Curly, you're gettin' off this coach. You're goin' back and ride with Whip Gleason."

The girl snapped out of her abstract to regard him curiously.

"Why, Hal? Don't you know—I want to ride beside you—all the way to Carson—"

Wade swung off to the ground, purposely keeping his gaze from darting up the hill to where he had seen the flash of sunlight on metal.

"Come on—hurry. Maybe you own these Wells Fargo crates, Curly, but I'm giving the orders. Come on!"

Frowning with wonderment, but too heart-weary to protest, the girl climbed down and walked back to where Whip Gleason had pulled up in the rear of Wade's coach.

"What's the matter, Hal? Sniff a dry-gulcher?"

Wade's piercing glance made the old jehu break off.

"Listen, Whip. You keep your stage here for fifteen minutes. I'm going on ahead. And I'm going to be inside that Concord, driving through the boot curtain. If you hear three shots, it'll mean I'm down on the desert, in the clear. If you don't hear any shots, turn your wagon and hightail it back to the top of the last hill where you got a good view in all directions."

Without further explanation for his warning, Hal Wade made his way back to the Concord, unwound the lines, and strung them under the curtain of the boot.

Then he climbed inside the stagecoach. From the front seat, piled with bundles, he could see through a slot in the front panels and guide the team along the road. In this fashion he would not present a target for the ambusher—if ambusher it was—who was crouching behind the mesquite up the hill.

The team started up, gaining the top of the ridge without difficulty. Below them were a series of switchbacks leading to the floor of the desert.

Peering through the slot under the boot, looking past the ears of the leaders, Hal Wade had a view of the purple desert, the tawny sandhills, the chocolate-brown pile of Shoshone Butte which had once held ambushed killers in the guise of Piute Indian warriors.

He saw no sign of danger, but he intended to drive his stage a full half mile before giving the safety signal to Whip Gleason and Curly Joyce. He knew that once out of the Badlucks, their danger of being bushwhacked would be over.

Wade's precautions were not unnecessary.

Lying on his belly behind the mesquites far up the hillside, Scorchy Langlie was watching the proceedings through powerful field glasses. Redfern's ace stage driver was unaware that the glint of sunlight on the polished lenses of the binoculars had been the reason why Hal Wade had deserted the driver's seat of the Concord and had climbed inside to do his driving.

"Won't do him any good whether he's inside or out, once that dynamite lets go under this wagon," grunted Langlie, as he saw the jouncing stage-coach vanish over the rise.

Langlie swung the glasses back to study the second Wells Fargo coach. Whip Gleason and Curly Joyce appeared to be arguing about starting up, Gleason shaking his head obstinately and keeping his brake lever set tight.

Casing the glasses, Langlie crawled back through the brush until he reached an arroyo which cut the top of the ridge. He had been posted on the east slope to watch out for the approaching stagecoaches and make his report to Redfern, ambushed on top of Shoshone Peak. In the event that a large posse was riding with the outbound Wells Fargo expresses, it was Langlie's duty to forewarn Redfern and Collier to hold their fire on the planted dynamite.

Scrambling at top speed down the slope, hidden from view by the arroyo's lava rims, Scorchy Langlie made his way to the foot of Shoshone

Peak. He got a glimpse of Hal Wade's stagecoach, now halfway down the grade.

It looked uncanny, to see a lumbering Concord bouncing along the ruts on its thoroughbraces with no visible driver in the seat. But the taut lines revealed that Hal Wade was keeping the team under control from within.

Clambering up the north face of the low cinder cone, so as not to be visible to Hal Wade from the stage road, Langlie arrived at the brushy summit, fagged for breath.

Collier, Redfern, and Rex Joyce waited behind the rampart of rocks, peeping through a tangle of brush at the Wells Fargo stage that was working its way down the switchbacks. Pegleg and Flannagan had been sent back to the Lucky Lode, hours earlier.

"What's up?" demanded Redfern, his fingers on the trigger of the .30-30 which was to set off the dynamite blast. "It looks like nobody's drivin' that stage, from here!"

Langlie gasped for breath, and grinned excitedly. "Don't worry. Wade's inside there—reckon he got leery about passin' the spot where those Injuns jumped him, so he got inside. Made Gleason and the girl wait at the foot of the ridge."

Redfern seized the field glasses from Langlie and focused them on the stagecoach, which was in the act of vanishing into a rocky cut at the foot of the hill.

The powerful glasses showed Redfern what he wanted to see—Hal Wade's hands and forearms, projecting out from under the canvas curtain of the boot, maintaining a taut grip on the leather ribbons which controlled his six-horse team.

A moment later the stage had lumbered out of sight into the cut, and Redfern handed the glasses back to Langlie.

"He's inside, all right!" panted the outlaw. "Wade's about to start on the slick skids to hell."

Behind the kneeling outlaw at the trigger of the rifle, Curly Joyce's father braced himself, intending to lash out a kick which might make the tense-nerved outlaw pull trigger inadvertently and set off the murderous blast prematurely.

But Black Bill Collier, watching the oldster intently, foresaw Joyce's plan and leaped to block the move, shoving the white-haired captive back into the brush.

Redfern's eyes glittered with fiendish suspense as he saw Hal Wade's stagecoach emerge into the open, the team breaking into a trot as they headed out into level ground.

Less than a hundred feet from the mouth of the cut was the innocent-appearing sandy stretch where hidden dynamite waited.

Sweat leaked from the faces of Langlie and Collier, as they watched the stagecoach horses trot on.

Now the leaders were trampling above the

dynamite cache, hoofs inches from grim destruction. Next the swing-span horses in the middle of the team—then the wheelers.

Two seconds, and Hal Wade's stagecoach was directly above the dynamite trap!

With a hissing intake of breath, Bret Redfern squeezed the trigger of the .30-30 Winchester wedged in the split rock.

The roar of the rifle was drowned in an ear-splitting crash of sound.

Down on the desert flat, a geyser of red fire and flying earth erupted under the moving stage.

The Wells Fargo coach seemed to fly into a million pieces, wheels and paneling and trunks and bundles of freight flying to all points of the compass.

The team was reduced to hash meat by the blast that opened a twenty-foot crater in the road. High, high in air lifted the shattered remnants of a stagecoach blown to smithereens. And a hundred-foot column of smoke and dust swooped up to hide the sun.

—Chapter XXXVI—

Death Rides with Destiny

In the appalling second of time that the outlaws flinched involuntarily before the tremendous thunder of the explosion, old Rex Joyce knew his only chance at escape had come.

Though his arms were tied behind him, the old man could run. He did so now, leaping unnoticed toward the rim of Shoshone Peak as the trio of owlhooters lifted their faces to watch the fountaining débris which soared heavenward, watching for a glimpse of Hal Wade's mangled corpse.

With a prodigious running broad jump, Rex Joyce leaped over the rocky parapet and fell twenty feet before his wide-spread legs dug into the roof-steep slope of Shoshone Peak.

His legs pounding, Joyce skidded and bounded like a scared antelope toward the desert flats below.

"We got to get Joyce!" yelled Bret Redfern, leaping to his feet and drawing a Colt .45. But the outlaw chief's words were inaudible to the eardrums of Scorchy Langlie and Black Bill Collier, so terrific had been the volume of sound from the exploding case of dynamite.

Yet the two realized that Rex Joyce must be stopped. They had intentionally let the old man witness their fiendish death trap, knowing they would kill him anyway. Now, with Joyce fleeing madly down the slope, he must be stopped before he made his escape and lived to tell what he had seen.

But even as Bret Redfern sprang to the top of the split rock which held the smoking, tied-down .30-30, he saw Joyce vanish behind the rolling tidal wave of brown smoke and dust flung mushroom-shaped along the ground by the explosion.

"Come on, men!" yelled Redfern, waving the other two forward over the wall of boulders. "We've got to tally that old son before that other stagecoach shows up."

Like soldiers emerging from a fortress, Collier and Scorchy Langlie vaulted the rock nest and started down the steep slope of the cinder cone, their high-heeled boots gouging long parallel tracks in the powdered lava.

Arms windmilling to maintain their balance, the three outlaws slid at breathless speed to the foot of the low volcanic cone, then paused to recover their breaths.

Redfern waved his two henchmen to separate right and left, eyes probing through the sifting dust and dynamite fumes to trace their escaped captive.

But Rex Joyce was nowhere to be seen. He was making the most of the curtain of smoke, getting as far out of gun range as possible before the screen of settling dust thinned out to reveal him.

The three owlhooters skirted the yawning hole in the ground made by the blast. Of the Concord stage, there was not a visible trace except in the junked matchwood and scrap iron flung for a hundred yards in all directions.

Vaulting over a quivering mass of broken bone and crushed muscle that had been a wheel horse, Bret Redfern stared down into the smoke-filled crater torn out by the explosion, in the thought that Rex Joyce might have dived headlong into the hole to seek refuge under the choking fumes.

"He'd have headed for that cut in the foothills," panted Redfern, running toward the southeast. "He can't be far—"

Dimly, through thinning smoke, the outlaw saw a running form. He whipped up his six-gun, then checked his trigger as he recognized the bannering coattails of Black Bill Collier.

From somewhere off to the left came the sound of two quick shots.

Redfern swung his gaze, sought for and found Scorchy Langlie. The old stage driver was standing still, fifty yards off to the north. A Peacemaker was bucking and thundering in his grasp, as Langlie fired off toward the southeast.

Gun in hand, Redfern sprinted toward Langlie. The jehu had evidently spotted the fleeing Joyce.

Then Redfern skidded to a halt, as he saw Langlie stagger under the terrific impact of drilling slugs. Beyond the pall of dust came two sharp whipcracks of sound.

"Joyce . . . didn't have a gun!" gasped Redfern, his short hairs rearing stiff on his neck nape. "And his hands were tied—"

Staring, Redfern saw Scorchy Langlie buckle at the waist, then pitch headlong to the ground, his smoking .45 dropping from nerveless fingers.

Redfern raced toward his fallen henchman, unable to believe his eyes. Who was shooting from the base of the foothills?

Then, off to his right, came the high-pitched yell of Black Bill Collier. His words reached Redfern's ears, still ringing from the roar of the explosion.

"It's Wade! It's Wade!"

What Redfern saw jelled his veins, paralyzed his trigger finger.

He saw Black Bill Collier, crouched like the professional gunman he was, firing in mad haste at a stalking figure that was emerging from the cut where the stagecoach road knifed through the lowest of the Badluck foothills.

Firing alternately with right and left six-guns, Collier seemed to be making a frantic, last stand against that approaching phantom.

It was the identity of that phantom that paralyzed Bret Redfern, in that insane moment of disbelief.

It was the tall, angular figure of Hal Wade that was striding forward, six-guns in hand, while Collier's bullets sang like attacking hornets on all sides of him. Stalking relentlessly forward, getting into sure gun range while the lantern-jawed gambler wasted his shots in wild confusion.

It was Hal Wade. There was no doubting that. But Redfern's brain told him that could not be. Wade had been aboard that shattered, annihilated stagecoach. It was impossible that Wade could be alive.

Fifty feet in front of Black Bill Collier, the cowboy from Arizona halted.

His six-guns came up, leveled ominously. Hammers dropped on firing pins. Twin jabs of orange flame winked from the .45 bores. And those flames were the last things that Black Bill Collier saw this side of eternity!

Chest and skull riddled by expertly-aimed lead, the black-coated gambler staggered backward.

Then Collier's knees turned to rubber, and he fell on his back with sightless eyes staring at the smoke-mottled sky.

Festering hate seethed through Bret Redfern's veins then. The bullets that had cut down his henchman were real enough.

And Redfern, never the man to buckle and turn tail in a shoot-out, whipped up his own six-guns with hands that were as steady as rock.

Redfern's guns thundered in unison. Bullets kicked sand against Hal Wade's bullhide chap wings, as the cowboy turned to face his enemy a hundred feet away.

Bracing himself against the expected shock of lead, Hal Wade extended his right arm in front of him, squinting eyes peering down his gun sights as he staked all on one cool, deliberate aim at Bret Redfern's chest.

The .45 leaped in Wade's grasp.

As the wind cleared away the founting smoke from his hot-barreled weapon, Wade saw Bret Redfern drop his gun to claw instinctively at the gushing blood which poured from his breastbone.

Thumbs cocking his fuming guns once more, Hal Wade came grimly forward as he saw Redfern struggle to remain standing.

But death was contorting the outlaw's face. He dropped to his knees, his head jerking forward on his chest.

With the splayed fingers of his right hand trying to stem the torrent of blood from his riddled chest, Redfern groped an arm toward his fallen guns in the dust.

Then he jerked spasmodically and pitched forward to slam his twitching face into the dirt. There was no sign of life when Wade's shadow fell across the sprawled form of his fallen enemy.

A yell tore Wade's attention from the corpse of Bret Redfern, and the cowboy looked up to see old Rex Joyce scrambling awkwardly out of the smoking crater which marked the grave of the last Boothill Express ever to head into the desert wastes.

Holstering his guns, Wade waited until the old man had lumbered to his side, his gait awkward because of his trussed arms behind his back.

Taking a knife from the pocket of his chaps, the Arizonan severed the oldster's bonds, and then the two were shaking hands above the limp and lifeless body of their foe.

"I figgered to make a break for it and maybe warn Curly and Whip," panted Joyce, "but I never figgered you'd help me get out of this alive."

Wade laughed, his eyes surveying the débris-littered desert about him.

He pointed at the nearby cinder cone.

"That fake Indian raid came from that hill," he said. "So instead of remaining inside that Concord, I tied the lines tight and hopped out and slammed the door shut, when the stage was passing through the cut back there. That's why Redfern thought I was aboard that Boothill Express when he blasted it to hell."

The two were walking slowly back toward the foothills when they spotted Curly and Whip hurrying on foot over the summit above them.

They met midway up the stage road, and for a moment Curly Joyce and her father clung to each other in the ecstasy of their reunion.

"What happened over here?" demanded Whip Gleason, his diminutive form fairly dancing with impatience as the girl disengaged herself from Rex Joyce and was caught in Wade's arms. "We heard one hell of a bang, and came runnin', knowin' Hal must have run into an ambush. What become of the stage?"

Hal Wade, pulling the girl's spun-copper curls against his shoulder, winked at Joyce.

"You explain things to Gleason," the Arizonan said. "I got to spend a few minutes arranging to make you my father-in-law."

He looked down into the girl's eyes.

"There's no reason now why Wells Fargo can't start off in business again, back in Deadhorse," the cowboy said. "And I'm hankerin' for a job of stagecoachin', if one's open."

Curly Joyce pulled his head down to the level of hers and pressed her cheek against his.

"You're hired," she whispered. "But how will you feel taking orders from a woman boss, after you being a boss yourself on the Rocking R?"

Hal Wade laughed.

"I won't feel sheepish workin' for a Wells Fargo outfit that has a girl for its boss," he told her, "so long as that girl happens to be named Mrs. Hal Wade!"

Center Point Large Print
600 Brooks Road / PO Box 1
Thorndike, ME 04986-0001 USA

(207) 568-3717

US & Canada:
1 800 929-9108
www.centerpointlargeprint.com